Branded Outlaw

SELECTED FICTION WORKS BY
L. RON HUBBARD

FANTASY
The Case of the Friendly Corpse

Death's Deputy

Fear

The Ghoul

The Indigestible Triton

Slaves of Sleep & The Masters of Sleep

Typewriter in the Sky

The Ultimate Adventure

SCIENCE FICTION
Battlefield Earth

The Conquest of Space

The End Is Not Yet

Final Blackout

The Kilkenny Cats

The Kingslayer

The Mission Earth Dekalogy*

Ole Doc Methuselah

To the Stars

ADVENTURE
The Hell Job series

WESTERN
Buckskin Brigades

Empty Saddles

Guns of Mark Jardine

Hot Lead Payoff

A full list of L. Ron Hubbard's
novellas and short stories is provided at the back.

*Dekalogy—a group of ten volumes

L. RON HUBBARD

Branded
Outlaw

GALAXY
PRESS

Published by
Galaxy Press, LLC
7051 Hollywood Boulevard, Suite 200
Hollywood, CA 90028

Printed in the United States of America.

ISBN-10 1-59212-258-2
ISBN-13 978-1-59212-258-5

Library of Congress Control Number: 2007927518

Contents

Stories from Pulp Fiction's Golden Age

A ND it *was* a golden age.

The 1930s and 1940s were a vibrant, seminal time for a gigantic audience of eager readers, probably the largest per capita audience of readers in American history. The magazine racks were chock-full of publications with ragged trims, garish cover art, cheap brown pulp paper, low cover prices—and the most excitement you could hold in your hands.

"Pulp" magazines, named for their rough-cut, pulpwood paper, were a vehicle for more amazing tales than Scheherazade could have told in a million and one nights. Set apart from higher-class "slick" magazines, printed on fancy glossy paper with quality artwork and superior production values, the pulps were for the "rest of us," adventure story after adventure story for people who liked to *read*. Pulp fiction authors were no-holds-barred entertainers—real storytellers. They were more interested in a thrilling plot twist, a horrific villain or a white-knuckle adventure than they were in lavish prose or convoluted metaphors.

The sheer volume of tales released during this wondrous golden age remains unmatched in any other period of literary history—hundreds of thousands of published stories in over nine hundred different magazines. Some titles lasted only an issue or two; many magazines succumbed to paper shortages during World War II, while others endured for decades yet. Pulp fiction remains as a treasure trove of stories you can read, stories you can love, stories you can remember. The stories were driven by plot and character, with grand heroes, terrible villains, beautiful damsels (often in distress), diabolical plots, amazing places, breathless romances. The readers wanted to be taken beyond the mundane, to live adventures far removed from their ordinary lives—and the pulps rarely failed to deliver.

In that regard, pulp fiction stands in the tradition of all memorable literature. For as history has shown, good stories are much more than fancy prose. William Shakespeare, Charles Dickens, Jules Verne, Alexandre Dumas—many of the greatest literary figures wrote their fiction for the readers, not simply literary colleagues and academic admirers. And writers for pulp magazines were no exception. These publications reached an audience that dwarfed the circulations of today's short story magazines. Issues of the pulps were scooped up and read by over thirty million avid readers each month.

Because pulp fiction writers were often paid no more than a cent a word, they had to become prolific or starve. They also had to write aggressively. As Richard Kyle, publisher and editor of *Argosy,* the first and most long-lived of the pulps, so pointedly explained: "The pulp magazine writers, the best of them, worked for markets that did not write for critics or attempt to satisfy timid advertisers. Not having to answer to anyone other than their readers, they wrote about human beings on the edges of the unknown, in those new lands the future would explore. They wrote for what we would become, not for what we had already been."

Some of the more lasting names that graced the pulps include H. P. Lovecraft, Edgar Rice Burroughs, Robert E. Howard, Max Brand, Louis L'Amour, Elmore Leonard, Dashiell Hammett, Raymond Chandler, Erle Stanley Gardner, John D. MacDonald, Ray Bradbury, Isaac Asimov, Robert Heinlein—and, of course, L. Ron Hubbard.

In a word, he was among the most prolific and popular writers of the era. He was also the most enduring—hence this series—and certainly among the most legendary. It all began only months after he first tried his hand at fiction, with L. Ron Hubbard tales appearing in *Thrilling Adventures, Argosy, Five-Novels Monthly, Detective Fiction Weekly, Top-Notch, Texas Ranger, War Birds, Western Stories,* even *Romantic Range.* He could write on any subject, in any genre, from jungle explorers to deep-sea divers, from G-men and gangsters, cowboys and flying aces to mountain climbers, hard-boiled detectives and spies. But he really began to shine when he turned his talent to science fiction and fantasy of which he authored nearly fifty novels or novelettes to forever change the shape of those genres.

Following in the tradition of such famed authors as Herman Melville, Mark Twain, Jack London and Ernest Hemingway, Ron Hubbard actually lived adventures that his own characters would have admired—as an ethnologist among primitive tribes, as prospector and engineer in hostile climes, as a captain of vessels on four oceans. He even wrote a series of articles for *Argosy,* called "Hell Job," in which he lived and told of the most dangerous professions a man could put his hand to.

Finally, and just for good measure, he was also an accomplished photographer, artist, filmmaker, musician and educator. But he was first and foremost a *writer,* and that's the L. Ron Hubbard we come to know through the pages of this volume.

This library of Stories from the Golden Age presents the best of L. Ron Hubbard's fiction from the heyday of storytelling, the Golden Age of the pulp magazines. In these eighty volumes, readers are treated to a full banquet of 153 stories, a kaleidoscope of tales representing every imaginable genre: science fiction, fantasy, western, mystery, thriller, horror, even romance—action of all kinds and in all places.

Because the pulps themselves were printed on such inexpensive paper with high acid content, issues were not meant to endure. As the years go by, the original issues of every pulp from *Argosy* through *Zeppelin Stories* continue crumbling into brittle, brown dust. This library preserves the L. Ron Hubbard tales from that era, presented with a distinctive look that brings back the nostalgic flavor of those times.

L. Ron Hubbard's Stories from the Golden Age has something for every taste, every reader. These tales will return you to a time when fiction was good clean entertainment and the most fun a kid could have on a rainy afternoon or the best thing an adult could enjoy after a long day at work.

Pick up a volume, and remember what reading is supposed to be all about. Remember curling up with a *great story*.

—Kevin J. Anderson

KEVIN J. ANDERSON *is the author of more than ninety critically acclaimed works of speculative fiction, including The Saga of Seven Suns, the continuation of the Dune Chronicles with Brian Herbert, and his* New York Times *bestselling novelization of L. Ron Hubbard's* Ai! Pedrito!

Branded Outlaw

Chapter One

L EE WESTON'S big hands clenched tightly around the handle of the spade. For a little while he could not continue and then, taking a breath that held the shudder of grief, he began to scoop thick red gumbo into the grave, covering the body of his father.

It was done, and the two mesquite sticks he had tied together with a rawhide thong in the form of a cross cast their shadow across the raw, ugly earth.

Lee Weston dropped the shovel and turned to walk with weary gait back to the heap of still-smoking ashes which had been his home. There was nothing left there. Not even the frame which had enclosed his mother's picture had survived.

As he stood staring at the broken corrals and the ashes where the barn had once stood, his hands strayed to the guns on either thigh and his palms went up and down against the walnut, as though they itched.

His young face was a haggard mask and his blue eyes plumbed the depths of hell. Three weeks of riding, enough to kill a weaker man, three horses dead under him and now—this!

He remembered the letter in his pocket and he drew it forth. The chill morning wind rippled the stained paper.

Son:

I wish you could come back, if only for a little while. I realize that you are making money and a name for yourself, and I know that you probably still think that I was unduly hard on you at times, but believe me, my boy, when I say that I need you.

The day of the small rancher in Pecos Valley is over and the combines are moving in with better stock and more capital. Men, because of their money, think that they can buy a thing for which other men have given their lives.

Some day my part of this range will be yours. I have tried to keep it for you, son. But now I need help. Harvey Dodge, whom I once knew on the old Chisholm Trail as a raider, has come here.

Please do not fail me!

Your father,
Tom Weston

Lee put the letter back in the pocket of his batwings. The name Harvey Dodge was scorched into his sight so that everywhere he looked, the letters danced before him as though they were written in flame.

His strong mouth hardened into a bitter line. Three horses dead and three weeks of hell—and he had been only hours late! He looked at the hoofmarks in the churned earth and saw that at least twenty riders had made this raid. If he had arrived before their attack, he would probably now be dead. But he wasn't thinking of things like that. He was thinking of only one thing—of finding Harvey Dodge and pouring twelve slugs into him.

He had often thought of coming home, but never had he dreamed that it would be like this. Smoking ashes and dead men—those three sprawled riders, who might have been friend or enemy, he did not know which.

Coming home, with the acrid smell of powder smoke still lingering in the air. Coming home, and finding that he had no home.

He turned to his mount, intending to ride away. But the horse stood in deep dejection, lather dried upon his flanks and eyes glazed with weariness. Lee took the riata from the horn and walked out to the small band of broncs which had escaped from the corrals. He dropped his noose over the head of a buckskin who had not run away with the rest. Even the horses had changed here, but Lee Weston had been away for six years.

He saddled, forgetting that he himself was ready to drop from fatigue. He saw no ashes now, no mound of earth. He saw only the blazing letters that spelled Harvey Dodge.

Wyoming had hardened him, and Lee had every reason to feel confidence in his ability to even this score.

He did not take the wagon road to Pecos. He had a better way. Quirting the buckskin, he headed straight across the valley, down ravines and across gullies, sending the white dust swirling as he streaked through the sage.

He knew but one way to settle this, and until it was settled he knew that his mind would be hazed by the cold rage which had come into him with his first glimpse of the smoking ruins.

He guided his running horse into the main street, the only street, of the desert cow town. The place was hardly alive, though it was an hour short of noon. A dog yelped and fled out of the sun. A handful of loafers on the porch of the general store sat up, startled by the sight of the lone puncher who drew up and was immediately hidden as his own dust caught up with him. When the yellow fog cleared, the loafers stared appraisingly at the stranger's rig and, by riata and saddle, knew that he came from the north.

Lee spurred the buckskin closer to the porch. "Can any of you tell me where I can find Harvey Dodge?"

An ancient looked intently at him and then removed a pipe from his toothless mouth. "Say, now, ain't you Tom Weston's boy? Tom was in town last night. I reckon you'll find him out at his spread."

"Tom Weston is dead," said Lee. "I'm looking for Harvey Dodge."

The old man shook his head, wisely avoiding any taking of sides in what he immediately saw as a coming feud. "Reckon you better ask Tate Randall. He's sheriff here now. That's his office down the street."

Lee swept his cold glance over the men on the porch. They fidgeted, but took their cue from the old one.

"Much obliged," said Lee heavily. He swung down and led his horse toward the low 'dobe structure, half office and half jail, which housed law and order in Pecos, New Mexico.

A leather-faced, sun-dried individual with a star on his chest was drowsing over a stack of reward posters, waking up occasionally to swat at a fly which buzzed around his ear. But the instant a shadow appeared in the door, Tate Randall, through long and self-preserving habit, swiftly came to life, one hand half stretched out as a welcoming gesture and the other on the Colt at his side. His bleached eyes squinted as he inspected Lee.

"Say! You're Lee Weston!"

"Right," said Lee.

"Thought you was up in Wyomin' someplace havin' a hell of a time for yourself! Bet old Tom'll be plenty pleased to see you again. Used to stand down by the post office and read us your letters whenever you wrote. I thought—"

"My father was killed last night. The house was burned and the stock run off. I'm giving it to you straight, Randall. I'm looking for Harvey Dodge."

"Huh? Why, man, you must be loco! Harvey Dodge came in and bought the biggest spread in the valley. He's probably the biggest rancher in these parts now. *He* wouldn't do nothin' like that!"

"I'm still looking for Harvey Dodge."

Tate Randall stood up and shook his head. "Sonny, I've burned enough powder to run a war, and I've shot enough lead to sink a flatboat. If I had it to do over again, I'd use my head and let the law do the findin' and shootin'. If you go gunnin' for Dodge without any more evidence than you've got, there's only one thing that'll happen to you. We'll be building a scaffold out here to string you up. Now think it over. You'n me can ride out and look over this killin' and then—"

In disgust, Lee, turning, started toward the door. But it was blocked by a smooth-shaven, rotund gentleman in a frock coat. Lee saw eyes and hands and thought, "Gambler!"

"What's up, Tate?"

"Doherty, like to have you meet Lee Weston, old Tom's boy."

Ace Doherty extended a be-diamonded hand, which Lee took doubtfully.

"Doherty," continued Tate Randall, "this young feller is about to go on the gun trail for Harvey Dodge. You can back me up that Harvey ain't in town."

"No, he's not around," said Doherty dutifully. "You've got Dodge wrong, youngster. He wouldn't pull any gun tricks, like killin' your old man."

"I don't recall telling you that my father was dead," said Lee.

"Heard it at the store," replied Doherty. "Well, cool him off, Tate. You're the law and order in these parts." He walked away.

Lee faced Randall again. "It's all right to try to cut me down to size, but there's only one thing that counts with me right now, Randall. Last night about twenty men jumped my father. He wrote me his only enemy here was this Harvey Dodge. I'm talking to Dodge."

"Well," shrugged Randall, "if you don't trust justice, you don't trust it, that's all. Trouble with you gunslingers—"

"I don't happen to *be* a gunslinger."

Randall grinned thinly, looking at the well-worn Colts on the younger man's thighs. "Maybe I heard different."

"Maybe you did," said Lee. "But in Wyoming, it hasn't been fixed yet that courts and sheriffs can be used by crooks."

"Maybe you'd better take that back, son."

"I'll reserve judgment on that. But everybody is taking this too calm. The whole town has known for hours what happened out on the Lightning W, and you're still sitting here!"

He ignored the sudden challenge in the old gunfighter's eyes and turned his back upon him to stride out into the hot sunlight. The first thing he noticed was that the street was deserted, even to the loafers on the porch of the general store. He tensed, seeing that a puncher had just led a favored bronc well out of harm's way.

Lee's steps were measured as he approached his buckskin. But things were far from right. He felt a cold chill course down his spine, and turned to face the porch of the Silver Streak Saloon. A thickset man was standing there, arms hanging loosely level with his gun butts. He was unshaven and dirty, but for all that, there was an air of authority about him.

"You lookin' for Dodge, fella?"

Lee came to a stop. "Got anything to offer?"

"Yeah," drawled the man on the porch.

And then it happened. Like a snake striking, the fellow's hands grabbed guns. Lee leaped to the right, flipping his Colts free. Thunder roared from the porch, and then Lee hammered lead through the pall of smoke which drifted between them.

A pair of boots dropped into sight under the white cloud. Slowly the gunman sagged to the earth, both hands clutched across his stomach, still holding his guns. He made one last effort to fire, but the shot ploughed dust. He lay still.

Lee saw doors swing wide on the other side of the street. Three punchers leaped forth, taking one startled glance at the dead man and then grabbing for their guns.

Across the way, another door opened, to show the muzzle

of a Winchester. Lee saw that he had too many on too many sides. He jammed his toe into the buckskin's stirrup and swung over. Shots crashed and a slug almost ripped him from the saddle. Another struck, and his leg went numb.

Valiantly he fired toward the punchers, making them duck for an instant. He dug spur and sped down the street, the Winchester making the air crackle above his head.

Hanging grimly to his horn, his face white with strain, he guided the running buckskin out into the prairie and then north, toward the hill that loomed blue in the distance.

Lee knew that he had only started. The man on the Silver Streak porch had been too young to be Harvey Dodge. He knew that he had just started, but with his life pouring redly from two wounds, he knew that the chances were high against his ever finishing anything but living.

Chapter Two

GRADUALLY the proximity of death drove all other thoughts from Lee's head. He rode in a red nightmare of pain, fast because he could see the cloud which marked the pursuit behind him. Somehow he had to get into the mountains.

Many times, as a boy, he had ridden over this terrain. And it was only because he knew it so well that he was able to reach the canyon mouth which led upward into a tangled labyrinth of ravines and peaks. Somewhere ahead, he knew, there was a stream and on its banks there was an old trapper's cabin, so well hidden that few punchers, interested mainly in the flat range, had ever come upon it. That place, where he had once spent happy weeks fishing for trout, was his only chance of life—providing he could remain conscious long enough to reach it.

The miles of rough canyon trail fell behind him. The air became crisp and scented with the pines which whispered in the mountain wind. He found the divergent game trails, well knowing that one mistake in direction would be the end of him now. He climbed the torturous ridges and somehow paced the buckskin down the rockslides.

Ahead he could hear water running. But it was masked in

pines and he could not yet be sure if it was the right stream. And then a flash of brawling silver water came to him and he knew that he was right.

Another problem began to gnaw into him. He had no medical supplies. For a long while he would be unable to hunt his food. With a chill he realized that he was not proceeding into his salvation, but into slow death by starvation!

Once, while prospecting, he had uncovered the moldering skeleton of a prospector who had been overtaken by a storm. He remembered how those hollow sockets had stared at the blue zenith never to see again. Would he too be found someday, guns rusting at his side, scattered by the starved wolves . . . ?

His arms were numb with the ferocity of his grip on the pommel. He could barely lift his head to see if the cabin was still there. The vague outline of it crossed his senses and then, his will to live exhausted, he slipped quietly out of the saddle and to the cushion of pine needles. Consciousness was slipping away from him when he heard a step.

Had he come this far only to be trapped anew? Weakly he tried to reach for his guns, but he could not find strength enough for the effort. In despair he sought to focus on the being who approached.

It was no shock to him that it was a girl. Nothing could shock him now. Behind her was a grizzled old puncher with hostile eyes.

Lee saw the girl lay down her trout rod and come nearer. He had a vague vision of hair which held the sunlight, soft hands and hip boots. And then the sunlight began to spin madly and he could see nothing but murky red blackness, thick stuff in which he was drowning. He knew no more.

Ellen Dodge opened his shirt and looked at the wound in his chest. A Western girl, brought up on the range, she was not unused to violence. And so it was that her reaction was mainly one of pity rather than fright or horror.

"Get some water, Buzz."

The old-timer scraped at his thick, dusty beard and squinted a rheumy eye. "If I was you, Miss Ellen, I wouldn't go pokin' my head into what was none of my business. I ain't never seen this jasper before, but he's wearin' two guns and them batwings says Wyomin'. He don't belong here and he ain't up to—"

She stood up and stamped her foot. "Buzz Larsen, I believe you'd let your own mother die for fear of getting into trouble. Now get that water and don't be all day about it."

Obediently, Buzz took a canvas bucket and went down to the creek. Ellen hurried into the shack for a first aid kit and came back just as Buzz was about to empty the bucket on Lee's head.

"Buzz! Haven't you a drop of mercy in your veins? It's kinder to leave him unconscious. There's a bullet—"

"Lord," said Buzz. "You got more nerve than anybody I ever see. You mean you're goin' to take that bullet out like you did on that horse you shot?"

She didn't answer, already at work.

"Never see the beat of it," said Buzz, puzzled. "Anythin'

that's ailin' shore puts you to work. There's goin' to be trouble about this, you just wait and see. I feel it in my bones."

She proceeded efficiently with her work and, at long last, completed the bandaging.

"Take his head and we'll carry him inside."

"How do we know we won't be harborin' a criminal?" said Buzz.

She gave the old man one look and he hastened to do her bidding. Together they carried Lee into the ramshackle cabin and laid him on a pile of clean blankets. Tenderly the girl covered him.

"He's so young," she said. "He couldn't be bad, Buzz."

"Yeah? Listen here, young lady, that's when they're wusst. When I was his age I was burnin' powder up and down the Mississippi and becomin' the terror to all beholders. I recollect one time—"

"There's somebody coming," said the girl tensely.

Buzz's gun-deafened ears were slightly slower in picking up the sound, but at last he did so. "Must be fifteen, twenty of 'em. And they're lookin' for somethin'. I told you so, Ellen. This here jasper ain't—"

"Buzz Larsen, if you say one word about his being here, I'll . . . I'll . . ."

"I wish you'd finish that threat sometime, miss. You got me plumb ragged with suspense."

"One word and it's your life," said Ellen darkly. "When that young man is strong enough to get around, then they can come after him. But it would be murder to give him up now. And besides, I don't think he's done anything."

"That party sure is searchin' the trail," said Buzz, still listening.

They went out into the clearing and watched the narrow aisle between the pines where the riders must appear. At long last, Tate Randall, leading the others single-file, came riding into sight, ducking his scrawny head to keep the branches from knocking his hat off.

Randall was very pleased to see Ellen Dodge. He lifted his hat and bowed. "Howdy, Miss Dodge. How's the fishing luck?"

"Very good," said Ellen. "I didn't think anybody knew about this place except maybe Buzz and I."

"We tracked a feller up here," said Randall. "Shore beats . . . Beg pardon, ma'am. It's curious how much blood a feller can lose and still keep ridin'. He's signposted his trail for fifteen mile. You ain't seen nothing of anybody but us, have you?"

"You mean another rider?" said Ellen.

"Yes'm," said Randall. And behind him the posse sat up straighter, scenting the kill.

"Why, Buzz and I were way up the stream until just a moment ago. Buzz, didn't you hear somebody runnin' a horse up Moose Canyon about an hour ago?"

Buzz swallowed hard and avoided all eyes. "Yes'm."

"Then that must be the man," said Ellen. "You go straight up this stream about three miles and then you'll see a big pine with the top blown out of it. You turn down that canyon, and I guess maybe you'll find his trail again."

"Thank you!" said Randall. He started to quirt his mount but hauled in again. "Say, I don't reckon he's dangerous by this time, but if you see him, don't take no chances. He's Suicide Lee Weston from Laramie, and he just shot and killed John Price."

Buzz gave a start. "Y'mean," he gulped, "that this feller *killed John Price*? Was it a even break?"

"Far as we know," said Randall. "But a couple others got in the road of slugs and that's murder as far as the law's concerned. Keep your eye peeled, Larsen."

"Gosh," said Buzz. "I mean, I shore as hell will! John Price! The fastest man in Pecos!"

Randall lifted his arm in signal and spurred off, the others pressing close behind him, each man with guns ready.

Ellen watched them go and her mouth was tight with scorn. "They call themselves men!"

"What's wrong with that?" said Buzz. "This feller must be hell on skates with a gun. Say! We better call them gents back. Maybe this Weston is after the Triple D outfit in full."

"John Price was a fool and a braggart."

"That don't make no difference. I never liked him neither, but that don't change the fact that he was yore old man's foreman. Golly, what's goin' to happen next! I told your old man he was a fool ever to move into this range. I told him . . . What'd he say this ranny's name was?"

"Suicide Lee Weston," said Ellen. "But I don't believe it."

"Weston," mused Buzz. "Say, there's a Weston spread, the Lightning W, over across the valley. And if I recomember correct, there was a Weston that used to gun whip yore dad's men regular when and if caught down on the old Chisholm

Trail. You don't suppose the feud's goin' to open up again, do you?"

"I'm sure there's some mistake," said Ellen. But she did not look so sure for all that. Her small, sun-tanned face was troubled as she went back into the cabin.

She sat on the edge of the table, one boot swinging, and looked for a long time at the motionless man in the corner. Slowly the frown cleared away and she smiled sympathetically. "He's too good-looking to be bad. Don't you think so, Buzz?"

"Women!" said Buzz.

Chapter Three

DURING the ensuing two weeks, three Triple D riders were successful in finding the crumbling cabin on the bank of the trout stream. And three Triple D riders were greatly amazed when the ordinarily hospitable Ellen failed to ask them to take so much as a drink of water. And because it was a long ride back on empty stomachs, each one of the trio reported very sourly to Harvey Dodge.

To the first's suggestion that Ellen might be up to something, Dodge returned an abrupt, "Nonsense." To the second, he said, "I hardly think Ellen would cook anything up."

But when the third man returned, stating, "Boss, she's plumb set on stayin' where she is. If you ask me, I think that Weston jasper is someplace around and she's protectin' him. You know how Miss Ellen is. And besides, I seen a buckskin hoss out in a pasture right close to the cabin."

Dodge stood up from his roll-top desk. He was a craggy-browed old man, bristling with white hair and made sober by countless brushes with the grim reaper.

"She never did mind worth a damn," said Dodge crossly. "But by God, this is going too far. There's a pack of coyotes skirmishing around this country and that Weston is still on the loose and I refuse to keep havin' nightmares about her.

If a man was to chop down on him, Buzz Larsen would run a mile. Tell Pliney to saddle up my Piedmont. I'll bring her back myself!"

Dodge got into a tweed jacket and buckled a six-gun around himself, muttering the while at having to quit his ranch house just when work was piling up thick and fast.

He drove the Piedmont hard, anxious to get back before night, and with the big animal's long legs pushing the miles under him, he followed the directions given him and, by two in the afternoon, galloped into the clearing.

Because one rider had just been there, Ellen was not on her guard. And Buzz had found a shady spot on the bank of the stream and gone to sleep.

Lee Weston was mending with the miracle speed of a youth whose entire life has been one of hardship and outdoor work, and for the past several days he had been taking a very keen interest in his benefactress. He considered her a most remarkable woman in more ways than one. She was so persuasive and usually so right that no argument would prevail against her. For three days now he had been insisting that he was well enough to travel, and just now, watching Ellen clean up the luncheon dishes, he renewed his argument.

"Ma'am, I was thinking that if I stayed here much longer, I'd plumb wear out my hospitality. You been so good to me that I know doggone well I'd never be able to repay you if I was to find a million dollars."

"You can repay me by keeping still about leaving," said

Ellen, standing beside the bunk and rubbing a tin dish with a towel much longer than was absolutely necessary.

For some time he had been considering telling her just how he came to be wounded. She had asked no questions, had volunteered no information. But now he saw that she was really running a danger in case he was discovered there, no matter who she was—a fact which he did not possess.

"Ma'am, I'd be a yellow dog if I didn't tell you that maybe it ain't any too smart to keep me around these diggings."

"Nonsense."

He sat up, bracing himself with his elbow and plucking at the blanket to avoid her eyes. "Maybe I'm not all you think I am, ma'am."

"Maybe I don't consider it any of my business."

"But it is your business. If you'll listen, I'll tell you how come I dropped in on you in such a state."

"You needn't."

"I used to use this as a fishing cabin when I was a kid," said Lee. "And so I knew pretty well how to get here and supposed I'd be safe. When I was around this country, I was the only one that knew about it. Well, to make it short, I come rolling into the Lightning W—" He stopped, suddenly silenced by the enormity of the remembrance. His face went hard and the girl, watching him, suddenly perceived that there were merciless depths in him which she had not suspected. It frightened her a little.

He found himself again. "My dad wrote that a man named Harvey Dodge, an old enemy of his, was moving in on the valley. Dad was scared, bein' old and short-handed. He sent for me. And . . . and when I got home . . ."

"Don't go on if it hurts you," pleaded Ellen, seeing an entirely different side to him now.

"The place was all shot up and I must of went sort of crazy. I blasted into town and yelled that I'd get this Harvey Dodge and all of a sudden I was in the middle of kingdom come. And so I came here. I'm wanted, most likely. And I'll hang if they catch me, even break or not. So maybe you better let me go."

"Has it occurred to you that you may be wrong about my—about Harvey Dodge? After all, that's very slim evidence on which to shoot a man. Harvey Dodge may be hard and he may be a bit strange at times even . . . but I don't think he would do such a thing."

"That's all I've got to go on," said Lee.

"Then you'll continue even after what they did to you in Pecos?"

"Yes," said Lee. "I have to do that."

"Please, Lee, hasn't there been enough killing over cattle and grass? Not all of this valley is worth the life of a man."

"You know my name?"

"Yes. And I know more than that. You are on the wrong trail. The law has taken over the right of Judge Colt to settle problems for cattlemen."

"The law," said Lee bitterly. "I've run into law before. Judges you could buy for a dime, juries that return the verdict to the most guns, sheriffs that hang on to the side with the most votes. Don't talk to me about law."

"Maybe she won't," said a hard, brutal voice in the doorway. "But I will."

Ellen whirled to see her father and the tin plate clattered to the floor. Lee barely moved.

Thumbs hooked truculently into his gunbelt, Dodge walked halfway across the room and stood staring at Lee.

"So you're Weston. Suicide Lee Weston. Ellen, get out of here."

She had been frozen with surprise, but now she stepped in between them. "No. No, you're not going to touch him! You can't! I didn't bring him back to life for this!"

"I said get out," repeated Dodge.

She had never seen him so terrifyingly hard, and the hand which thrust her to one side came near to being a blow.

Lee's voice was smooth as silk. "Go ahead and shoot, whoever you are. I don't seem to have any guns around me. You're safe."

The tone and manner came as a shock to Dodge. He had seen and heard it many times before. Long before when the Chisholm Trail furnished rich prey to those young and bold enough to dare try for it. It was Tom Weston who lay there in that bunk.

"You don't know me," said Dodge. "But I'm the man you was spoutin' you was going to get. My name is Dodge. Harvey Dodge."

"Go ahead and shoot," said Lee, apparently bored.

"I'll shoot when I'm ready, and that won't be long. You've come back here to drown Pecos Valley in hell. It's not going to happen."

"Very simple," said Lee. "You have the solution under your hand. You got my father on an old grudge and now you've got me."

"That's a lie!" stormed Dodge. "I didn't kill Tom Weston, though God knows I should have a long time ago. I came to this valley peacefully. I was willing to let bygones be bygones. And then my first herds are cut into ribbons, my best horses stolen, a puncher shot. And I knew. But—"

"So you killed an old man to pay off a score thirty years dead. The trail was wild and men died easy or hard and you run into one man you couldn't whip. And so you cook up an excuse at this late date to pay him off. It's plain, Dodge. Plain enough for me and plain enough for anybody. And if you don't shoot me now you'll live to regret it."

Buzz stole in the door and stood staring at Ellen, mouthing, "I tole you there'd be trouble!"

"But this scrap is between you and me," said Lee. "This girl is evidently your daughter. She didn't know who I was. She took pity on a gent whose luck had run out and—"

"I knew who he was," said Ellen. "I knew what he did. And I'd do it all over again."

"I'm dealing with you later," said Dodge. "Go on outside."

"You're going to kill him!"

"I'll let the law do that."

"But it was an even break!" she cried. "And John Price started it!"

"Take her out," said Dodge to Buzz.

Buzz reluctantly forced the girl through the entrance and

out into the sunlight. With his heel, Dodge slammed the door shut.

"Make one move toward your gun," said Lee calmly, "and I'll blow you through the wall."

Dodge stopped, astounded, watching Lee pull back the blanket and show the six-gun which rested its muzzle on the bunk rail.

"Shuck your belt mighty careful," said Lee. "They can't hang a man twice."

Sullenly, Dodge unbuckled his gun and let it slide to the floor. Lee climbed out of the bunk, somewhat dizzy when he stood up but his Colt never wavering as he dressed. He fumbled for his boots and found them. Awkwardly he drew them on. He stiffly buckled his gunbelts about him with one hand and then pulled his batwings from their hiding place under the table, throwing them over his arm.

"She's your daughter, isn't she?" said Lee.

"Sure. What of it?" challenged Dodge.

"God does some funny things," said Lee. "But it ain't for me to ask questions. If I was you, I wouldn't talk up to her about this. She's been doing what she thinks is right. I'm doing what I think is right and maybe you do too. But we just don't agree somehow and there seems to be just one way to settle this argument now."

"I'll settle it," said Dodge grimly. "I'll give you some advice, Weston. Clear out of this valley and don't ever come back. You don't own anything here and I've got plenty of guns waiting for you."

"So I don't own anything," said Lee.

"I've closed down through the bank. The Lightning W is mine."

"You're pretty obvious, Dodge. Murder, theft . . . Isn't there any place where you draw the line?"

"You'll eat those words someday, with lead around them."

"It takes more than one to make a feast, according to the Sioux. This is my inning now. Maybe you'll have yours later. But there's one thing I can tell you and tell you straight. That's too nice a girl to have hangin' around a pack of thieves. The only reason I didn't let you grab iron was her. I can't kill you and then expect her to want me the way I want her. That's my problem and I'll figure it out. And you can thank her for your life. Remember that when you think maybe you'll get tough with her about this."

Walking unsteadily across the room and watchfully around Dodge, he opened the door.

"Buzz, saddle my horse."

"Lee!" cried the girl incredulously. And then, in the same instant she turned, half expecting to see her father dead. But Dodge was standing with scowling face just inside the door.

In a moment, Buzz brought the buckskin up. Lee found it difficult to mount, but at last he made it, holding himself erect with the pommel, gun still trained on Dodge.

"Goodbye, Ellen."

"Won't I ever . . . ?"

"I'll be back," said Lee. "Yes, I'm sure of that."

She held his stirrup for a moment, looking up at him, wondering how he could ever live if he tried to go through the mountains in the north. But she knew his resolve and somehow she could not find it in herself to question any decision he might make.

"Goodbye, Lee."

He neck-reined the buckskin into the trail and spurred into a trot, conscious of the mixed feelings with which they watched him go. He could almost feel the relief in Buzz.

Chapter Four

NEWS travels swiftly in the West and before a month had gone, there lived not a magpie that had not heard about Lee Weston.

A minor shooting scrap, born out of rage and the desire to somehow atone for the loss of a home, enacted in the comparatively sleepy town of Pecos became a full-sized battle in the mouths of men who had only news and tall stories with which to pass their evenings. Generally they combined the two and now the result was hardly to be recognized.

It seemed that a man named Suicide Weston, already tallying so many lives that he had stopped cutting notches to save his guns, had decided to take over all of Pecos Valley single-handed and had practically succeeded until the United States Cavalry had thrown a division into the place and then the troopers, combining forces with the New Mexico Rangers and civilian posses had only been able to slightly wound said Suicide Weston who, through the help of a Mexican woman passionately devoted to him, managed a complete escape.

So grew the stories of Masterson. So grew the stories of Holliday. So grew the story of Suicide Weston. In Wyoming the residents distinctly remembered eight shooting scraps involving Weston, each one of the proportions of a Custer's Last Stand.

Nothing had happened for a long, long time. The idols of the six-gun sagas were peacefully pushing up prickly pear in company with their victims and the time was ripe.

Men calculated, with much labor and little evidence, that Weston could have downed Hickok on an even break—though some demurred and said that Hickok might have stood a fairly good chance. Here and there a gunman, his own pride piqued by the sudden growth of this seven-day wonder, muttered into his whisky that *he'd* like to meet this Weston. *He* wasn't so hot.

Frontier marshals polished up their Colts, each thoughtful of his own repute, and looked wise when the name Weston was mentioned.

Lee, all alone in the fastnesses of the New Mexico ranges, was completely unaware of his sudden fame. He knew the facts. He had evidently killed two men besides John Price while standing exposed in the middle of the street. He only knew that he would have to go back and settle the score with Dodge sooner or later.

But Lee was wise enough to refrain from entering any towns. In the first place his chest felt stiff, thus impeding his draw. In the second, he had not a dime. Theft never entered his head, even on the day when he used his last Winchester cartridge to bring down a buck deer.

Hopes were never lower than Weston's on the night when he skinned that deer. He sat by the jumpy light of his fire in the shelter of a tall rock, morosely wondering how it was that a man could talk so big even when he knew he could do so little.

Dodge had power. He could hire half a hundred gunslingers

if need be. Dodge had the law all on his side—a fact which was all too apparent in the actions of Tate Randall in Pecos. And Dodge had further protection—Ellen.

Three loads of bullets for his six-guns and he was through. He could jerk this meat and perhaps live on it for six weeks. After that he could kill his horse and live on that. After which he would be able to concentrate only on one thing, the search for food. And sorry it would be, that search. Perhaps an occasional trout, a few roots . . .

Angrily he finished the skinning. Why the hell didn't he go down to Pecos and shoot it out and have it over with? He'd be dead, certainly, but then wasn't dying that way better than skulking here in the mountains, facing death by slow starvation?

He put a venison steak on crossed willows over the coals and the fat began to sizzle and drip into the fire. And each time a drop exploded in a bright ball of light, Lee's shadow went leaping gigantically up the boulder behind him.

Something changed in the sounds of the night. For a moment he could not place it, and then he knew that the buckskin had stopped pulling up grass at the end of his tether.

Lee came to his feet in a crouch. He slid sideways to get out of the blaze. In a little time he saw the buckskin, ears up, staring into a clump of pines below. The starlight was not sufficient to tell him more.

He hung in the darkness, waiting, listening, trying to cast his mind out from him to search that clump of pines. At last the venison recalled him to the business at hand. It was beginning to blaze brightly on one end.

"Some damned panther," he decided in self-justification and crept back to his fire to salvage his meat.

Expertly he turned over the willow grate by grasping the ends. But the instant he started to replace it, thunder crashed in the ravine. Hot coals, startled into blazing, leaped from the fire. The shot hit a cooking stone and screamed as it glanced away. Lee jumped back, losing the steak entirely to the flames.

Guns drawn, hunched forward to stab a shot at anything that moved in the darkness, Lee waited, raging over his lost dinner and at his helplessness.

A stone dropped, bouncing down the side of the boulder. Somebody was above and somebody was below. It was quite plain that he was completely surrounded. But he had no thought of giving up.

A voice came out of the dark. "Drop your guns."

"Come on and get them!" challenged Lee.

A Winchester answered. Lee ducked behind a clump of brush.

"Walk out of there with your hands up!" came the command. Lee was silent.

From five sides flashed a volley, lighting up the night. Bullets swarmed like wasps through the brush about Lee.

And then the voice came anew. "Come on out or we'll let you have it this time."

Lee did not move.

There came an interminable wait while Lee hoped he could figure out which one had ruined his supper for him. He'd get that one first and the others later.

"We can see you! Come on out!"

But again Lee had no answer.

Another pause ensued and finally the patience of the men, smelling venison and seeing the uncut meat and hungering also for the cheerfulness of that fire which burned all by itself in the night, wore out completely. A hardy soul got up from his hard couch and cautiously began to walk forward, eyeing the clump so generally that Lee knew he had not been spotted.

Lee let that one approach the fire. The fellow had a tattered red shirt with a bib front and a flat, floppy hat which marked him as a railroad crew man.

Presently another, seeing that the first was still alive, stood up from behind a rock and came forward mincingly, ready to cut and run at the first sound of strife. He was a Mexican, a bright but dirty serape thrown over his left arm and shoulder, the better to shield himself if it came to knife fighting.

Then a small shower of rocks avalanched down the face of the boulder and a rotund man whose proportions were not instantly appreciated until it was seen that he towered over his companions, tobogganed into view. He had a very fancy sombrero and his guns were set with silver and, all in all, if he had not been so travel-stained, he would have been *muy hidalgo*.

The other two also scouted the ground and came forward. One was a puncher of sorrowful aspect and drooping mustache and the other was apparently an easterner as he wore a derby hat and a bright checkered vest—both stained and ripped.

The quintet were somewhat nervous, trying to pierce the gloom which overlay the shrubs.

"Aw, what the hell, Pete. I got him. Saw him go down myself." This from the railroad man.

"*Señor,*" said the small Mexican, "I call you one liar. *I,* Felipe, saw my bullet take him just over the heart."

"Can it," said the man with the derby. "Let's eat."

The big, onetime gorgeous Mexican jerked his thumb at the clump. "Steve, what you think about running over and getting that feller's guns and money."

"I'll bring in the guns myself," said Lee.

They were shocked into immobility. They dared not look around. They had laid aside or holstered their weapons.

Lee stood up, a gun in each hand, walking slowly forward. "I take it that you gentlemen are hungry."

"*Sí,*" said the big Mexican. "But, *señor,* forgive us. We had thought you were a very bad fellow who did us great harm. We have made a mistake and we apologize from the depths of our souls." He started to remove his sombrero to make a sweeping bow.

"Stand up!" said Lee. "Before you could pull that knife from your shoulder, you'd be dead."

"Knife?" said the big Mexican. "*Señor,* you wrong me! I, *don* Jose, would never dream of such treachery."

Lee turned him around and relieved him of the knife. "All right, gentlemen. You want food. I need ammunition. Shall we sign the armistice and swap?"

"Certainly!" cried *don* Jose. "I give you all the ammunition we can spare. We accept your gracious invitation to dinner." He indicated the other four. "May I present Felipe the Road Runner, Big Steve, Brandy Bill and Sad Sam Pettingill. My worthy compatriots. And . . . ?" He paused, waiting for Lee to announce himself.

Lee was doubtful for a moment and then saw that fate had assigned him to such kind. "My name is Weston."

Suddenly *don* Jose sank down on a boulder and hid his great face in his greater hands, rocking to and fro. "Angels of mercy! Saint Ignacio! *Madre de Dios!*" He stared at Lee. "Forgive me! Forgive me!" He turned on the railroad man. "Steve, by all the gods, have you no eyes? Cannot you recognize even such a one as Suicide Weston?" And to Lee. "*Señor,* accept my humble apologies from the depths of my soul, claimed though it may be by Satan. If I had only known!"

Suddenly *don* Jose sprang up in wild, gesticulating excitement. "Comrades! The keg of molasses and the corn meal! Felipe! Spit the meat and do it well. Sad Sam, you will sing! Today we are honored! Today the gods are good to us. Today we have met Suicide Lee Weston!"

The others looked at *don* Jose in stunned silence, and so did Lee. He was not quite able to credit himself with such extravagant fame. But, slowly, he holstered his guns, eyes still on *don* Jose.

And the instant the guns were in their leather, something round and solid prodded Lee in the back hard enough to break his spine. A hissing, baleful voice said, "Grab sky, Weston. I got a weak thumb."

Lee knew better than to turn. He elevated his hands with all the others looking at him. And then *don* Jose broke into a guffaw which shook the peaks about them.

Felipe scuttled forward to lift Lee's guns and search him for a hide away.

"Get some rope," said the man behind Lee to Big Steve.

Steve got the required riata and dropped it around Weston's shoulders, pulling it tight, tying it and then fastening his wrists together.

With a shove, the sixth member of the crew sent Lee sprawling beside the fire. Lee rolled over and stared up at the gambler Doherty, whom he had met in Tate Randall's office the morning of the fight.

"*Señor* Doherty," said *don* Jose, "this is a pretty good joke, yes. But what do we want to tie him up for? If we don't want him, we kill him. If we do want him, then we want him with us."

"Shut up, you fool," said Doherty matter-of-factly. He sat down on a rock and made a motion for the others to start getting the supper together.

"It's a good thing I lost you guys in that canyon," said Doherty. "None of you've got the brains of a beetle. Here you got four aces and the king of spades and you was willing to throw a feast for him."

"He's a great gunman," said *don* Jose with a shrug. "Why not?"

"Because I got other ideas, that's all," said Doherty. "We need money and we could stand some public approval."

"Money?" said *don* Jose. "But how? He is worth most with us."

Doherty pulled a tattered sheet of paper out of his pocket. "You guys are all blind. All five of you passed this without even bothering to read it. But me. I've got the brains around here. I pulled it off the tree and now . . . read it."

Don Jose pursed his lips and scowled as he spelled the letters painfully out.

"'Five thousand dollars reward will be paid by Harvey Dodge for Suicide Lee Weston alive. Three thousand dead. Signed Sheriff Tate Randall, Pecos, New Mexico.'"

Don Jose smiled widely, displaying gold teeth. "Ah, yesss. I theenk I understand, *señor* Doherty. But," he shrugged, "it is a pity to lose such a man. How will you deliver him?"

"I'll take him in myself," said Doherty. "The rest of you can wait. Harvey Dodge is going to pay cash and Tate Randall will be set for the next election. And that makes me better lookin' than a royal flush to all concerned."

Doherty looked down at Lee. "Thanks, pardner."

Chapter Five

TATE RANDALL sat pruning his fingernails on the shady side of the jail, his chair tipped back against the 'dobe and his mind a few leagues away. A hound was scratching sleepily at its ear, rarely connecting but scratching just the same. A deep peace lay over Pecos—something on the order of the silence which surrounds a midnight murder.

Two horses came at a walk past the Cactus Theater and Tate casually looked up to see who it might be. Instantly he brought all four legs of his chair down into the dust and leaped to his feet.

Harvey Dodge and Ellen pulled in and Dodge sat glowering at Tate. The sheriff could not help wishing that the old man's temper was as good as the girl's. She sat a sorrel very calmly, her face shaded by a flat hat which was held to her curly brown head by a silver-caught chin thong.

"Randall," said Dodge heavily, "I've been meaning to talk to you."

"Come on in the office," invited Randall.

"This'll do just as well," stated Dodge. "I'm asking you here and now how long you are going to stand for a pack of thieves taking everything in sight over the whole of Pecos Valley?"

"Something else happened?" said Randall.

Dodge snorted. "Does something else have to happen to set you to work? I lost a small herd of steers night before last and one of my boys was winged. I sent word to you to come out and see about it."

"Yeah, I know," said Randall. "But I was over in Smokey Arroyo checkin' up on some stock that was run off from the Flying A. You ain't the only one that's getting it."

"But I'm the only one that isn't going to stand for it any longer," said Dodge. "This has been going on for weeks. Unless something is done I'm going to send to Arizona for a crew of gunfighters that can handle this thing."

"Looks like the crew you've got is tough enough," said Randall. "If you want to jump the law and try it on your own, all I can do is stand aside. There's only one thing I'd have to be sure about."

"And that?"

"Is whether or not you really was lookin' around for what you said you was."

Dodge eyed Randall with cold disdain. "You've been listening too hard, Sheriff."

"Maybe," said Randall.

"Things have been happening for four months," said Dodge, not caring to push the issue at the moment. "And I'm laying ten to one that a man named Weston is at the bottom of it."

"Started before he got here," said Randall.

"His old man was here, wasn't he? I could tell you a few things about old man Weston. And what was to prevent young Weston from bein' in the country weeks before he showed himself?"

"Yeah, I guess that's right."

"Sure it's right. If one or two things hadn't happened . . ." he glanced harshly at Ellen, "we wouldn't be havin' to put up with none of this monkey business. Good stock disappearing, probably into Mexico. Five or six dead already and more wounded. Night raids that don't leave a trace. The man behind that is smooth and that man is Lee Weston."

"Maybe you're right," said Randall.

Several townsmen had gathered in the street to listen in on the talk. And now one of them said, "Sure it's right. I been sayin' that for weeks. Ain't I, Bart?"

"Yeah, I guess you have all right," said Bart.

An oldster said, "He had a pretty tough rep up in Wyomin'. I got a letter from Ed the other day. Wasn't a man around there that wanted to stand up to him."

"You see?" said Dodge to Randall. "I'm not the only one that says Lee Weston ought to be strung up."

"I see you ain't," said Randall.

Ellen's face gradually lost its color as she stared at the faces in the crowd which began to increase about them.

Dodge looked steadily at Randall. "If you'll lead it, I'll organize a posse that won't miss findin' Weston this time."

Randall looked around and wondered about votes.

"What about it, Tate?" yelled somebody in the crowd.

Randall had to nod. "Sure, I'll lead it."

"Okay," said Dodge, "we're starting now!"

Men moved swiftly away to get horses. Tate Randall limped toward the livery stable. But just before he reached the door he heard a shout of astonishment in the street.

Men moved swiftly away to get horses.

He whirled and shaded his eyes to better see the three riders which were approaching.

The one in advance was hatless and seemed to be heavy in his saddle. On second glance Randall saw that the fellow's arms were tied. As the trio came closer Tate recognized Doherty.

"They got Weston!" bellowed a puncher in the street.

The crowd collected again to surge down the dusty road to meet the advancing party. Randall sped swiftly before them to get on the ground first.

Lee gave the sheriff a cool, unworried study. "That wouldn't be a lynch mob comin', would it?"

Randall glanced over his shoulder.

"You was whinin' about law," said Lee. "And now as long as I've got to play it your way, let's see what you know about justice."

The crowd was surrounding the trio.

"Stand back, boys," said Randall. "How are you, Doherty?"

"Aces against a full house," said the gambler, his smooth face wreathed in a grin. "You still sore about the way I was dealin' night before last?"

"Hell no," said Randall.

"Tell these rannies to get out of the way," said Doherty. "I got to deliver this jasper to Dodge." Both the gambler and Sad Sam were nervous at the sight and sound of the hungry mob which eddied around them, staring at five thousand dollars worth of bandit.

Dodge came spurring through the press. He reined in

before Lee. "So you didn't get away after all. We got something that'll cure you, Weston. A cure that's mostly hemp."

Lee was silent, looking the other way to keep from seeing Ellen.

"Did these posters mean what they said?" asked the anxious Doherty, producing one.

"You bet they did," said Dodge harshly. "Bring him along, boys."

With too many hands on the buckskin's bridle, progress toward the jail was slow. Lee listened to what the crowd was saying and when they arrived before the 'dobe structure, he gave Randall a humorless grin.

"Nothin' cheap about you, Sheriff. Looks like you've got a good way to clear up your whole book."

"Get down," said Randall.

A dozen pairs of hands dragged Weston into the street. Randall, still in command of the situation, hauled Lee up the steps.

Weston glanced back and saw that Ellen hovered on the outskirts of the crowd, her mount pacing nervously under the tension she put on the reins.

"Maybe we ought to string him up. Doc Benson'd be alive if it wasn't for him!"

Randall turned toward the voice. "Take it easy, gents. This man rates a fair trial just like any of you would. There's one thing funny about the whole affair. He wouldn't have killed his own father. Give him the benefit of the doubt for the moment anyhow."

"Wouldn't put it past him," jeered a puncher, brave with numbers.

Dodge was in the doorway as Lee went through.

"I've got you to thank for this," said Lee. "Sure ain't any limit to what money can do in the hands of a coyote."

"Go ahead and growl," said Dodge. "You'll be singing a different tune tomorrow."

Tate Randall pushed Lee into the office and closed the door. They were alone, though the mutter of the crowd came clearly to them.

"So you went bad," said Randall. "I wish you'd of listened to my advice when you came trompin' in here that mornin'. Know what they'll try to hang on you?"

Lee looked at the stringy old gunman with bleak distrust.

"You were right," said Randall, continuing. "The judge will clear the record with you. Where have you been?"

"Hiding out in the hills."

"You look rough enough," commented Randall. "Since you downed John Price, a couple thousand head of stock has turned up missin'. A rancher named Doc Benson was killed and his place burned. The Overland was stopped last Thursday and relieved of its bullion. Now you got some idea of what you face?"

"Plenty, isn't it," said Lee.

"Maybe you did it. Maybe you didn't. But men have funny minds. They'll start remembering that they seen you at each and every one of these crimes and they'll believe it, too. Now look, kid, you're hot-headed. You got plenty of sand and maybe I'm a damned fool but I half believe you and I'm going to do what I can to see that you get a square deal. I'll make the judge book you for that one killin' that everybody knows about and you can stand or fall by that."

"Square deal? With Dodge money talkin' loud?"

Randall chewed at his mustache. "Yeah, that's so. Well, I warned you, kid, and you'll have to take your chance. Walk ahead slow. The first cell on your right."

Chapter Six

LEE WESTON was a greatly worried and puzzled young man as he restlessly paced the cell and waited for the deep black to fade out into dawn.

To him it seemed that there couldn't possibly be an honest man in all Pecos Valley. He distrusted them, principally because of their unreasonable thirst for his blood before trial. He was thoroughly convinced that Harvey Dodge was the man behind the scenes in these reported crimes, but how could one man fight a crew like that of the Triple D?

Looking from his cell, the evening which had just passed, he had eyed the Triple D men as they wandered from bar to bar, taking a holiday to match the mood of their boss. Some of those men bore unmistakable stamps of lawlessness. Two of them he had recognized as having been requested to keep going from Wyoming. With an eye closed a man could still see that the Triple D outfit was as bedded with snakes as a lava rock in the sun.

Doherty, the bland-faced gambler, seemed to be part and parcel to the crowd as he was constantly in their company. And the men Lee had seen with Doherty had been unmistakable. *Don* Jose was known as a border outlaw.

All roads led to Dodge, no matter how hard it was to

reconcile Ellen to such company and parentage. And though, as he would soon discover, the premise was false, it was the only one on which he could operate.

His position seemed hopeless. His strong hands made no effect upon the iron bars of the window, and Tate Randall was too wise to take any chances with him. And Lee was steadily receiving new evidence for worry. It had long been his pride that he could keep his head while hell was popping loose, but now, facing a blank wall of despair, he was close to losing it.

All night long small groups of riders had been arriving from various parts of the valley to tether their mounts before the several saloons. And each time a group came out to stand in the half-light made by the lamps within the buildings, they eyed the jail as they swayed drunkenly.

Little by little, making a night of it, the riders' voices became louder and more excited.

At three o'clock, Tate Randall came to the jail. He inspected his prisoner with a glance and then went back to the front office where he began to put cartridges in the chamber of a Winchester. Evidently Tate expected some reinforcements in the form of deputies, as he continually paused to listen toward the rear door of the building.

This was the last straw to Lee. His young face was strained and his hands clutched the door bars. "What's up?"

"Nothing," said Randall. "Take it easy."

"I can hear them," said Lee. "They wanted to string me up yesterday, but they needed a spree to work them up to it. Are you going to stand up to them or just make a show of it?"

"Nothin's goin' to happen," said Tate. "Just talk."

Lee listened to the noise which drifted from the saloons. "What the hell's wrong with them? How do they know whether I'm guilty or not?"

"There's a heap of things been happenin' for the last few weeks," said Tate. "Don't blame 'em too much."

"I don't remember men like this in Pecos Valley when I was a kid," said Lee.

"Times have changed, son. We're gettin' all the driftin' scum of the railroads—and owl-hoot kids from the northern herd trails." He said this last with a meaningful look at Lee.

"Dodge sure brought himself a crew when he came," said Lee.

"He didn't bring it in," said Tate, busy loading another Winchester. "Them gents was already drifting around the country. Dodge didn't bring nothin' but his gal and a bankroll."

Lee frowned a little. He sat back on his bunk, rolling a cigarette to make himself concentrate. He lighted it from the bottled candle on the bench and inspected his smoke. The roar in the town was growing louder again and more men than before were coming out on the porches and staring toward the jail.

Lee went back to the door. "Look, Randall. Who's this gent Doherty?"

"Small-time tinhorn," said Randall. "I suppose you'd like to gun him for bringin' you in. Forget it. He needed the money."

"Yeah?" said Lee doubtfully.

In the street men were beginning to gather, talking excitedly, most of them too drunk to see single, but all of them getting mad *en masse*. Soon they all began to move in the same direction—toward the jail. There were over two hundred of them.

"Here they come," said Tate. "And every damned deputy gone over to 'em."

Lee watched the sheriff intently as the old gunman took up a Winchester and went to the front barred window.

A roar greeted his appearance. It had an ugly, animal quality which sent a chill coursing down Lee's back. He had never been caged before, had never felt so completely at the mercy of men.

"Stop where you are!" shouted Randall. "There ain't no hangin' party takin' place in Pecos tonight."

A chorus of jeers were hurled at the sheriff. And then a man stepped forward and, rocking drunkenly, shouted, "Give him up or we'll come and get him! We all know what he's done!"

It was Doherty!

Randall's answer was lost in the cheers which followed Doherty's speech. The crowd pressed forward again. Randall raced to the door and dropped the bar securely in place.

A moment later, shoulders were thrown against it. Nothing would stay that crowd now and Randall knew it. The old man stared at the buckling oak and then, turning to the table, picked up Lee's six-guns.

He came to the cell and unlocked it.

"You'll let me help?" exulted Lee.

"You're gettin' out of here," said Randall, handing the guns to his prisoner.

"You mean . . . you mean you're letting me go?"

"Yes, just that. Don't stand there jawin'. Get going before some of them remember the back door."

"But what'll they do to you?" said Lee in sudden concern.

Randall shrugged. "I'm afraid that's in your hands, son. Me, I don't figure you like the rest of 'em. Maybe because I don't believe all I hear. This'll cost me my job, unless . . ."

"Unless what?" said Lee, buckling on his belts.

"Unless you can do a better job of scarin' up the guilty party than I done. I ain't goin' to stand back and watch 'em hang a man that might be innocent."

The door was beginning to splinter. Lee stared at the sheriff and then shoved out his hand. "I'll do what I can, Randall."

"Get going," said the sheriff.

Lee ran to the rear door and slipped through it. Only one adventurous soul had come in that direction and he was too startled to do more than stop and gawk. When he did go for his gun, Lee's fist sent him sprawling into the dust.

Sliding into the shadow of the next building, Lee crept along, a little bit dazed by the suddenness of his release, and still failing to appreciate the real reasons which lay behind it.

He was about to head out and find a bronc when the thought struck him that not a few of those men were trained as government scouts. And again—he stopped and something like his old grin softened his face—again, who the hell would think to look for him in the town itself?

On the instant he sprinted through the shadows toward the livery stable. He could see the crowd still battering at the jail door as he rounded the last corner. The place was deserted of attendants. Everybody had gone mad at once in Pecos.

51

When he did go for his gun, Lee's fist sent him sprawling into the dust.

Lee seized the ladder to the mow and swung swiftly up it. He waded through the soft drifts of hay until he came to the cracked front of the building. He could lie there and see the street and, in addition, he could look through a pitching hole in the floor and command most of the stable's interior.

It took the unsteady crowd some time to knock down the door. They stopped just inside and a roar which swept back told the town that Weston was gone.

All their rage was concentrated immediately upon Randall.

But they weren't to do him any physical violence. Tate Randall had a small reputation of his own which was enough to stop that. What they did do was almost as bad.

Randall tried to talk to them, but they would not listen. They began to hurl insults at him, vying with each other to achieve lower levels of filth.

And as the minutes passed it became more and more apparent that Tate Randall's career of fifteen years' duration was ended then and there. The majority ruled.

Men began to scatter out in wide circles, hoping to catch the fugitive's trail. Others mounted and rode in a wide circle around Pecos. Still others stopped and speculated as to where the culprit had gone.

It went on for hours and as searchers came in, new recruits went out. By dawn the whole countryside was engaged in the hunt, combing the plains and ravines for any sign of Weston.

Little by little, Lee grew calmer. He promised himself that if he were discovered he would fight it out as long as he had bullets to fire and, after that, as long as he had strength to strike. He'd never give himself up to those madmen.

Despite the tension he was under, he had time to think. It was all so mad to him that Randall would actually let him go. And then he saw another reason beside mercy in the gesture which satisfied him. With Weston out of the way, the leader of the gang could cease operations without fear of final discovery. Of course that was balanced by the fact that Weston's release left the outlaws free to keep on. And here it was that Lee began to appreciate the sheriff's chance.

Unless Lee did something, old Tate Randall would never again be able to lift his head in Pecos Valley—or in the West for that matter. The man had staked his future on the possibility that Lee would stick to his guns and bring in the real leader. It made Lee feel better, that faith.

Carefully he sorted out possibilities. Of Dodge, now he was not so sure. The old man, having to pick a crew here, would take what he could get—the cast-offs from the other outfits in these high times.

Finally Lee's attention focused upon one man who was still very active, now at mid-morning, in keeping the town stirred up.

Doherty had brought him in. Doherty had evidently commanded that lynch mob, had probably started it himself, running the chances with his five thousand dollars to make sure that Lee failed to come to trial where he might state the company in which he had found Doherty.

Suddenly it all began to fit. Doherty had been in the sheriff's office that fatal morning. He had gone out and, immediately, John Price and some of the Triple D boys became anxious to get a possible menace to their schemes out of the way, never dreaming that their target was pretty good with targets himself.

Maybe Dodge fitted in. Maybe he didn't. But it was very apparent to Lee that the five men in the mountains and the Triple D crew were responsible for the raids.

That made his problem simpler. All he had to do was to somehow discover Doherty's hideout, get the real evidence and bring it back to Pecos. That would clear himself and it would reestablish Randall. Further, it would remove a danger from Ellen—and that danger was very real.

The hours dragged forward to noon and, at last, Harvey Dodge came in from his ranch to see if he could help in the search. He evidently did not intend to ride in it himself as he brought his Piedmont to the livery stable and, because the attendant was gone, had to unsaddle the horse himself.

Lee, above, watched the unwitting Dodge who fumed and rushed his rubdown, anxious to get into the affair.

Boot beats came from the front door of the stable and Lee saw Doherty entering. The man was rubbing lily white hands together and beaming as he approached Dodge.

"Shall we go over to the bank and get that five thousand?" said Doherty.

Dodge glanced up with annoyance. "I'm reminding you that the posters read, 'arrest leading to the conviction of . . .' And he sure as hell didn't stay long."

"That's got nothing to do with my end of it," said Doherty. "Can I help it if he got away?"

"I hear you led that mob," said Dodge. "And that's what made that damned fool Randall let him go. You wait until I see Randall!"

"No matter what I did," said Doherty, "I brought him in and I'm claimin' my money."

"Go ahead and claim. You brought all this off and he ain't convicted yet by a long ways. I wouldn't welch if you hadn't been the one that made Randall let him go."

"That's an alibi," said Doherty in an ugly tone. "I don't believe you've got the five thousand."

"I'll have it as soon as I send out my beef shipment to KC."

"You mean you're broke?" said Doherty.

"Broke?" said Dodge. "A man ain't broke with a hundred thousand dollars in land and beef. If Weston is caught and convicted, then I'll pay you that reward in addition to any other reward I have to pay. Is that all right?"

"No, it ain't all right," said Doherty.

Dodge turned his back on him and started to dump a can of oats into his Piedmont's manger.

So swiftly did it happen that there was no time to warn Dodge, no matter how suicidal that would have been for Weston. Doherty gave his arm a straightening motion and a Derringer fell from his sleeve into his palm. In the same motion he pulled the trigger.

The shot was thunderously loud. Dodge gripped the edge of the manger, trying to turn around, his breath knocked out of him and already out on his feet.

Weston saw his chance. He put a gun on Doherty from above. "Don't move!"

Doherty glanced up. The Derringer's second shot was sped almost before the words had left Lee's mouth. The slug sent splinters into his eyes and, though he tried a lucky shot, departing footsteps told him he had lost.

He knew only one thing. He had to get out of there before men came swarming into the barn. Doherty might be fool enough to spread the alarm and then try to shoot Lee before he could tell what he had seen.

Lee dropped down the ladder. His buckskin was in the stall on his right and he flung a saddle across the bronc's back. With feverish haste he got the bridle in place. Already he could hear people coming.

Swiftly he led his mount toward the back of the stable intending to use that door. Before he went through, he glanced back and gave a start.

Ellen was already halfway down the length of stalls, staring at Dodge crumpled up over the edge of the manger. She changed her glance to Weston.

"Lee!" she cried. "You've . . . you've killed my father!"

Jolted by her interpretation of it, Lee still could not pause. Others were entering the stable. He yanked the buckskin through the back door and hurled himself into the saddle.

A Colt banged behind him, swiftly followed by a volley. Men were sprinting for their own horses, bawling the news at the top of their lungs and sending the whole town into bedlam.

Plying his quirt, Lee streaked through the brilliant sunlight, cursing himself for the madness which had made him linger in Pecos.

And now, what would Ellen believe? Harvey Dodge, shot in the back, his own presence in the stable . . .

Now he was done for!

Chapter Seven

LEE had two advantages in that flight. The buckskin had been rested at the start and had been fed his quota of oats the night before, whereas the pursuing legion had already wearied themselves and their mounts in constant searching throughout the morning.

With the fiery sun blazing down upon his bare head and the hot wind cut by his lean face, Lee raced eastward, pulling into play his knowledge of the country by plunging into the first ravine he came upon and following its tortuous course until it branched. This put him out of sight for whole minutes at a time. The dry gullies were too stony to leave much trace of his going and, in the labyrinth of washes the men who followed found it necessary to pause precious seconds to again pick up the trail, only to see Lee come into view each time with a greater lead than before.

He steadily widened the gap beyond a Winchester's range and then, reaching a low rank of hills, went into a series of zigzags, each one of which removed him again from the path those behind thought he would pursue.

Within an hour he was able to ease up the lathered buckskin's pace. He chose a stony way and, by a circuitous route, came to the crest of a hill higher than the rest which overlooked the valley.

He could see from there that many of those in the hunt had already fallen out, taking pity on their horses. These straggled along, spreading out in the forlorn hope that the fugitive might double back through his pursuers.

Lying on his stomach, hidden in a pile of rocks, he occasionally caught sight of detached parties which had branched off on independent ideas of their own. But few of these came even close to the hill on which Lee lay, because of its position, so far to the right of the course to the mountains everyone supposed any man in his right mind would have taken.

He was hungry and weary with tension and now he began to be conscious of thirst. His position was bad enough without that. With the entire countryside in arms over the shooting of Harvey Dodge from the back, it was unlikely that men would ever grant him amnesty. And unless he somehow brought Doherty to justice, wherever he went he would be branded by the stigma.

If men had ever been convinced of his guilt in the valley crimes, they certainly were now.

And Ellen . . . The thought of how she must feel made him wince. More than anything else he wanted to prove to her that he was worth the care she had given him.

A haggard feeling of helplessness settled down over him as his physical discomfort increased. Without a rifle he could not hope to bag any game in the mountains. He could run the risk of killing a steer on the range, but he dared not stay near the herds.

Very late in the afternoon he was watching the parties

straggling back to Pecos in search of food and fresh mounts before they pushed their search into the mountains. In their state of excitement, he knew, they would waste no time on rest, but would probably start out that very night and dragnet the hills. Therefore, he dared not approach the fastnesses he knew so well. How completely he was trapped!

Only two riders were traveling in his direction now, too far away as yet to be identified. Evidently they were heading toward the Triple D. At long last he could recognize the barrel-bodied Buzz Larsen and then, finally, Ellen.

She rode listlessly, and Lee feared the worst about Dodge. He had to restrain himself from mounting and riding down to her to try and convince her that he had not done that thing. But it was too dangerous to move away from his position. He had no real way of knowing if any searching parties were still on the trails.

He watched her passing on the foot of his hill and his heart went out to her. How must she feel now with Dodge perhaps dead and with her faith in a man proven apparently false?

Lee watched her out of sight and then rested his head on his arm, trying to figure a way out of the tangle into which he had stepped a month before, and which had grown steadily worse with each passing day. He could not go anywhere without food. He dared not try for the mountains now and the range all about him was very dangerous. He had no ammunition, no blankets, no rifle and very few loads for his Colts. One solution was to ambush a segment of the searching party, but he recoiled from further violence unless it would lead straight to Doherty.

Doherty, that smooth-faced, tricky rat! Why the devil, thought Lee, couldn't a man recognize facts when he saw them? Doherty it had been from the beginning. But just now Lee's word was far less than Doherty's and so the actual shooting would be attributed to Lee even before a judge and jury—providing this excited valley would ever allow him to live that long.

It seemed to Lee that he was destined to lose everything he had or wanted. His father and his heritage in Pecos Valley, the only girl at whom he had ever looked twice, his reputation . . .

He sat up with a cold, bitter grin. Hell, he didn't have anything left. He couldn't lose no matter what he did or how he did it. And didn't he want to talk to Ellen? Couldn't he convince her, perhaps, that he hadn't shot Dodge? Well, then, the place to do that was at the Triple D. And there he could get guns and ammunition and blankets and food. Certainly none of the riders would be there in all this excitement. That was the last place on earth they'd look for him.

Or was it? Could he be sure the riders were gone?

He had to run that risk. Certainly he could not lie down here and give up the ghost. There was Tate Randall to think about.

It was dark when he rose and tightened the buckskin's cinch. Warily he led his mount down the slope, through the pinnacles of rock which stood like grotesque heathen idols against the stars, each one passing silent judgment upon him.

He was either going to salvation or going to the last battle of his life.

Chapter Eight

ELLEN was far from slumber as she lay in the four-poster, staring into the darkness, trying not to remember that Doc Franz had said Harvey Dodge had one chance in a million of pulling through. He had promised to send a rider the instant anything definite was known about either her father's condition or Lee Weston's fate. The doctor and Buzz had combined to coax her to return to the ranch. Anything might happen in Pecos just now.

A locust monotonously scraped his legs outside her window, making the only sound in the desert night. The open window shutters permitted the cool breeze to flutter the white curtains at her window.

She had never felt more lonely in her life. The world about her had been a violent one ever since the night her mother had died in St. Louis. And despite all his gruffness, there was a granite quality about her father and, sometimes, a tenderness even, which made his absence now seem like half her life was gone from her.

She hated to believe what she thought she had seen. The only other person in the world who had ever had her full interest was Lee Weston. And his defection was doubly hard upon her. If she had not saved his life, she told herself, her father would now be alive. And in trying to gain both she had lost both.

What she would do she did not know. This hard-jawed crew which her father had been forced to hire for want of men could never be controlled by one woman. She had rarely spent any more time at the ranch than she could help, because of the ranch personnel. She could often feel their eyes upon her and knew that they talked as soon as she was out of sight. She was not afraid of her ability to protect herself against them. John Price had once caught her wrist in the stable, to be paid with a quirt cut across his face. Probably that circumstance had greatly aided her forgiveness of Lee Weston there in the mountains. Certainly it wasn't a crime to kill a devil like Price. For a while Ace Doherty, dressed in his finest black broadcloth, had paid court to her, until he found that she was never in if she suspected that he was coming. Once she had left the message that she was ill and he, returning to town, had met her returning from a moonlight ride alone. She had wanted to beat him for his inference that she had returned just then from a rendezvous.

Earnestly she wished they had never come to Pecos Valley. The months they had been here had been filled with trouble and anxiety. Missing stock, arguments . . .

"God," she whispered into her pillow, "is there no peace to be found anywhere in this world?"

She thought she heard a footfall and raised herself a little to listen. The locust stopped his chirping and the wind troubled the curtains. Another sound came to her, a faint scraping on the wall. Somebody was examining the outside of the house.

She heard a shutter creak in the next room and started up to reach for the small .41 which hung on the wall. Her hand never reached it. Through the doorway stepped a man.

"Ellen. It's all right. It's me, Lee Weston."

She turned slowly, looking at him. Her heart was pounding in her throat, but she calmly lit the candle on the table beside her bed.

As its light leaped up to him she saw how gaunt and weary he looked and realized abruptly how much will there was in the man, who could keep going, even though he could not yet be fully recovered from those wounds.

Nervously he stepped to the foot of the bed, putting his hands on the rail. "Ellen, you've got to believe me. I didn't shoot Harvey Dodge. I was in the loft and saw it happen. Doherty did it and I dropped—"

"Please don't lie," she said, her throat tight.

"But Ellen! I'm not lying. God, won't anybody believe the truth anymore?"

"Why have you come here?"

"To tell you that. To ask for your help again. Tate Randall let me go and I promised I would turn up the man responsible for these crimes. But they're searching for me everywhere. I've got to have food and ammunition . . ."

"So that you can kill again," she said bleakly. "Go, Lee. I'll do that much for you. I won't tell them you've been here."

Lee regarded her for a long time without moving. She

was uncomfortable under that gaze and held the sheet more tightly about her.

After a while he turned and sat down on the windowsill. Slowly he built himself a cigarette.

"I can't blame you for believing everything that's said about me. It's true that I used my guns in Wyoming. But there's one thing you've forgotten, Ellen. Your father was too old to be feared on the draw. It wasn't necessary to shoot him in the back unless a man was afraid of him."

"Don't talk," she whispered. "I can't believe you."

"Is he still alive?"

"They wouldn't let me stay . . ." and suddenly she realized she was being drawn to him more strongly than she could resist, unless she refused further speech. "Go. There are half a dozen men here. Buzz guessed you might come to this place to try to get food and guns. . . ."

She stopped, staring at Lee and listening to a far-off rumbling sound which was swiftly growing louder, telling of the approach of a cavalcade of horsemen. Lee started up from the sill, throwing his cigarette out of the window and backing swiftly into the room. He glanced about him and saw that a closet was on his left, masked by a draped serape. Appealingly he glanced at her and then stepped into hiding, wondering whether or not she would sell him out, his hands on his guns indicating that he was fearful she would.

The riders stopped outside with a shout and dismounted to encircle the house. Somebody opened the front door with a crash and loud boots rang on the Mexican tile.

Buzz could be heard in loud protest and then the old man

backed up against Ellen's door, barring the way. "You can't go in there, I tell you. I won't let you!"

The sound of a fist meeting flesh and bone cracked and Buzz slid backwards through the opening door to stretch his length on the floor, a thick trickle of blood oozing from the side of his mouth.

Don Jose bulked gigantically in the entrance, gazing fondly at Ellen across the room. He came a few paces forward and then swept his sombrero from his head. *"Buenos noches, señorita."*

"What do you mean by this?" challenged Ellen.

"We have come for a few things we have forgotten," said *don* Jose. "A few thousand head of beef rounded up for us this afternoon, perhaps a little food, perhaps what money is in the house and," he paused with another dramatic bow, "and for *you, señorita.* My orders were very specific concerning that."

"You wouldn't dare!" she cried. "Who sent you?"

"A man most anxious to meet you. Shall we dress and go, *mi Americanita?*"

The drape swept back and Lee, a strange gleam in his eye, stepped into the room. *Don* Jose gave one glance and halted his hand on its way to his knife, bowing instead.

"The great Weston," said *don* Jose. "I had not expected to find you here!" He grinned. "Perhaps you come with us, yes?"

"Yes," said Lee, drawing with the speed of light, rolling both guns and dropping them into their holsters.

"Come, *señorita,*" said *don* Jose. "I shall withdraw while you dress, but be warned that men are outside to prevent your escape should you try."

It could only mean one thing to Ellen, that tableau before her. "Lee," she said in a heartbroken voice, all her hopes crashing to earth.

"Get dressed," said Lee tersely. "We'll wait outside. And don't be all day about it." He steered *don* Jose out of the room.

When the door closed she heard Lee say, "It did not take you long to get here, *don* Jose."

"Nor you," said the big Mexican. "I suppose we have you to thank for the killing of *señor* Dodge. You . . . ah . . . expect to be with us long?"

"I may or may not be," said Lee. He opened the door a crack. "Get some clothes on or we'll take you as you are."

Ellen saw the door close again and then wearily climbed out of the four-poster and reached for her clothes, seeing the uselessness of resistance. Only one precaution she took, and that was to hide the .41 inside her shirt.

She knocked on the door and it opened. Between Lee and *don* Jose she walked out through the house to the front steps.

A gasp greeted the appearance. Two or three hands went swiftly to guns, but others struck at the errant wrists. Men's eyes were very intent, watching to see what Lee would do.

But Lee paid no attention to them, helping Ellen to mount the horse they had saddled for her. Lee strode out to the stable and, from behind it, brought his buckskin and mounted. He rode back to the side of *don* Jose.

The whole crew, numbering thirty-five in all, but split because half of them were circling and beginning to drive the herds rounded up that day, was very doubtful about their policy toward Lee. They had no orders about him and each one was afraid to actively do anything on his own initiative. And besides, Lee seemed to be on good terms with *don* Jose. Stalled by their own confusion, they did nothing at the moment.

Ellen, looking about her, was startled to see that the bulk of these raiders were her father's own riders. Her heart was heavy at the thought of *don* Jose's inference that Dodge had died. And now she had nothing at all left in the world. Lee seemed so confident of himself here that she did not suspect that he was actually in danger of a shot in the back from second to each passing second.

They turned and, leaving a few to ride with Lee and the girl, most of them cantered out to pick up the herds and press them along. *don* Jose, attracted by beauty and curly brown hair, lingered.

"Where are you taking these cattle?" said Ellen at last.

"With open arms," said *don* Jose, "all Mexico awaits them." He swept his hand about him in a grand gesture. "Tonight we leave all this, thanks to *señor* Suicide Weston's activities. Tonight we shall march with swiftness and then pause to water the stock and rest as soon as the border has been crossed. There is a place in the mountains to the south—ah, you would never suspect it. A canyon which widens into green expanses, streams fed by springs, no way the place can be attacked, as it can be entered only through a narrow ravine which any one man of us could hold against a thousand riders. It is ideal, *señorita*. I am certain you will love it."

Now and then she glanced at Lee, detecting no strain in his face. He was riding as though he was quite at home with these fellows while, in reality, his ears were pitching for the sound of a hammer drawn stealthily back, or for the approach of one Ace Doherty who would, quite naturally, order Lee's execution the moment he appeared.

Chapter Nine

IT was near dawn when they reached the border, and the sun had just risen when the slow trek ended in the canyon rendezvous. It was just as *don* Jose had said and Ellen's heart sank as she saw that one man could indeed hold this place against all comers. The walls were sheer and one lone boulder beside the trail offered ample protection.

And she saw something else. Grazing on this expanse there were already several hundred Triple D animals, as well as great numbers of other brands. To this camp had come all the lost valuables in Pecos Valley.

They stopped before some low-built, mean cabins and she watched the others dismount. Lee got down with the rest, his face still unreadable and the attitude of the rest still very uncertain as pertained to him. The exaggerated importance given to Lee by the citizens of Pecos was bearing fruit in this extreme respect in a bandit camp.

Ellen, unable to do anything but connect Lee with these fellows, saw how grossly her father had been misled by the people about him. The Triple D had harbored the most of these riders. And who would have thought to look on such a spread for a band of outlaws? John Price had probably been their leader before he had died. And she had made the error of assuming that the killing had passed the leadership to Lee.

71

How else could she interpret this strange respect shown to him?

On *don* Jose's command she got down and went inside the first and largest cabin, one hand touching the .41 and very watchful for anything *don* Jose might do.

Lee stayed outside. He walked about, the others giving him a wide berth, still not knowing whether Doherty had actually recruited this man or not. They only looked in objection when he took a riata and roped a pair of fresh broncs out of the remuda. He was so very casual and certain about it that they hesitated to interfere.

Bringing the mounts back near the cabins, Lee changed their saddles. He was so aboveboard about it that he was still unmolested. But every fiber of his being was keyed as tight as a violin string. It could not be long before Doherty would come to them here and then . . .

He tightened the cinches and, boldly, kicked open the door and walked into the cabin. Ellen was standing against the far wall and *don* Jose was sitting in a chair building himself a cigarette. The big Mexican grinned when Lee entered.

"*Señor* Weston," said *don* Jose, "I am still wondering if Ace Doherty will approve of your joining us."

"Are you?" said Lee.

Ellen straightened up, suddenly seeing the other side of the situation and flaming anew with hope.

Lee kicked the door shut. *Don* Jose stirred restlessly.

"Stay where you are," said Lee quietly, "and you won't get hurt."

"What are you going to do?" said *don* Jose in sudden fright.

"Miss Dodge and I are about to take a morning ride. The horses are ready outside. Fresh horses, for which I must thank you. And you, *don* Jose, are going to come to the door and bid us goodbye and tell us to hurry back. Do you get that? And by the way, I'll take that knife from the back of your neck and your gun, if you don't mind. And remember that the first word of warning you give the rest will give you my first bullet. And I don't think you need any further evidence on what my guns can do."

"No," said *don* Jose swiftly.

Lee took the gun, but when he reached for the knife, the Mexican tried to strike. The blow did not land. On the contrary, *don* Jose landed on the floor and sat there rubbing his jaw. Lee put the knife into his own belt.

"Remember," warned Lee. He turned to Ellen. "Are you game to try this?"

Her throat was tight with emotion.

"Yes."

He let her go through the door first. Every man in camp stopped what he was doing and stared at the two as they came forth. This was going too far and there were angry mutters here and there, and more than one hand moved to gun butt.

But then *don* Jose was in the doorway, watching Lee and Ellen mount their broncs. And *don* Jose, haltingly it is true, was saying, "Hurry back, Weston."

"You bet," said Lee. "Come on, Ellen." And in a lower tone, "Ride as you've never ridden before in your life!"

Their quirts cut flank and the fresh mounts leaped ahead. They were running in a brace of seconds and it was well that they were.

"Drop them!" bawled *don* Jose. "Don't let them get away!"

Guns thundered behind them and bullets cracked about them. But they were moving too fast and were already too far away for Colts to be accurate. In a moment somebody would get a Winchester, but by that time Lee hoped to make the entrance to the hidden valley.

And then ahead of them they saw a horseman coming.

It was Doherty!

The man drew up in startled surprise, with no idea of who these riders might be, but knowing very well from the shots behind them and the sight of a riding skirt that all was not well. Doherty pulled in and grabbed for his own gun.

Lee fired straight ahead from the saddle. Doherty lurched. Lee fired again and the outlaw leader was slammed out of his saddle, his own Colt exploded toward the zenith.

And then Lee did a startling thing. He leaned out of his saddle and grabbed up Doherty by the front of his broadcloth coat and swung him over the pommel like a sack of meal.

Men were mounting behind them to give chase on fresh horses. There would be no advantage in broncs now and with the added burden Lee could not hope to outdistance them.

They raced through the narrow mouth of the pass. Just beyond it Lee pulled in, to leap for cover behind the boulder.

"Go get Randall. Get everybody you can and bring them here!" he shouted to Ellen.

*Lee fired again and the outlaw leader was slammed
out of his saddle, his own Colt exploded toward the zenith.*

She stared at him, halting. She saw that the boulder covered the pass on one hand, but it also covered the entire valley within from its opposite side. She knew how little chance Lee had, however, of holding that position.

"They'll kill you!" she cried. "Come on!"

"And lose them all?" shouted Lee. "RIDE! I'll be here when you get back—but for God's sakes, hurry!"

Irresolutely she started off again and then, realizing the need of haste, dug spur and raced out across the plains toward Pecos, knowing that nobody there would be squeamish about crossing the line where these bandits were concerned.

Lee shoved Doherty into a sitting position behind the rock and swiftly yanked his cartridge belt from him. Doherty, with a bullet in each shoulder, had no great taste for fighting now. But he glowered as he watched Lee stand up to breast the wave of riders which rushed toward him.

The outlaws saw him. A dozen guns cracked at once and they hurtled forward to ride him down.

Lee began to shoot with the cool deliberation of a man in a shooting gallery. Right gun, left gun, right gun. Over and over. Slowly, spacing and placing his shots with accuracy.

Saddles were emptied and the charging and now riderless horses charged onward. There was a swirl of dust where Lee stood, and then the horses were gone, and Lee was kneeling on top of the boulder with a Winchester snatched from a saddle boot and a cartridge belt of rifle cartridges obtained in the same manner.

Blood stained the stock of the rifle as he began to fire into the camp. Men were leaping for cover to lay down a hysterical barrage upon the rock, making a horizontal sleet of lead which screamed and yowled through the narrow passage.

Lee sagged once, his hand going up to a numb place in his left arm. And then, dropping lower, he resumed his firing, keeping the Winchester barrel too hot to touch.

Stone splinters lanced his cheek. A freak carom knifed him in the side.

Lee kept firing.

"Hurry, Ellen," he whispered against the thunder.

Chapter Ten

IT was sunset when the speeding riders of Pecos streamed southward toward the pass and came within sound of the firing. That guns were still going was enough to show that Lee was still alive, and for that Ellen sent up a thankful prayer.

Like an avalanche of fury, the Pecos men poured into the gap. If it had been held outwardly from the other side of the boulder, they could not have entered. But there was no defense now.

A tattered scarecrow of a man, grimed with powder smoke and white with loss of blood, stood staunchly behind the rock, still sending his shots into the valley after nearly seven hours of holding on.

Lee heard the men coming. He did not even look around. Very quietly the rifle slid out of his numbed grasp and he sank forward on his face without a sound.

Past him spurred the Pecos men, charging into the shambles of the outlaw camp with the lust for vengeance. But they found very little to attack now. The deadly raking fire had done its work. Eleven men were still on their feet—and lost little time in throwing up their hands, their nerves already shattered by the appalling accuracy of Lee Weston's shooting.

It was all over. Ellen put Lee's bloody head in her lap and pressed a canteen to his lips. He woke to the taste of water and drank greedily until she stopped him. He looked thankfully up at her.

"I . . . I was scared . . . you wouldn't get back 'til dark," he whispered. "That . . . would have been the end."

She held him close to her, crying softly and happily with relief.

Tate Randall loomed above them, dragging Doherty out of the place where Lee had wedged him. Doherty was in bad shape, and his morale completely shattered. He was ready to admit anything, if only they would keep Lee Weston away from him.

Tate knelt beside Lee, taking his hand. "You done it, son. I knew you would."

"I knowed he would too!" said Buzz triumphantly.

"How . . . how's Harvey Dodge?" said Lee.

"Doc Franz pulled him through. He'll be as good as new in six weeks. And Franz is here, ready to start in on you."

"Does he think . . . ?" began Lee. "That I . . ."

"Naw, hell," said Tate. "You shoot forty-fives and Franz took a forty-four Derringer slug out of Dodge. That spelt gambler and gambler spelt Doherty."

"Then . . . everything's all right," said Lee.

"Shore," said Tate. "Old man Dodge said to tell you that if you were still cussed enough to be alive, all that's yours is yours again and a hell of a lot more besides." Tate glanced at Ellen with a kindly smile. "And I think he bargained for more than he knowed," added Tate.

"Yes," whispered Ellen, holding Lee close to her.

Story Preview

NOW that you've just ventured through one of the captivating tales in the Stories from the Golden Age collection by L. Ron Hubbard, turn the page and enjoy a preview of *Six-Gun Caballero*. Join Michael Patrick Obañon, who's suddenly ousted from his spread by a band of criminals who falsely claim his ranch. Our *caballero*'s got to think fast to come up with a way to outwit his impostors when it's clear that it will take far more than mere guns to win the day.

Six-Gun Caballero

MICHAEL PATRICK OBAÑON was a handsome fellow. He had a graceful air about him and when he spoke he made poetry with his long-fingered hands. His voice was controlled and gentle and his glance was friendly and frank. For all the world he appeared not Irish but a Castilian gentleman from the court at Madrid.

Many hoofs, dulled by the sand of the yard, came close and stopped.

Michael stood up.

"Where are you going?" demanded Klarner, staring first at Obañon and then at the silver-mounted revolver which hung holstered from a peg on the wall.

"To ask them in, of course," replied Michael, unconcerned.

Klarner caught at the leg-of-mutton silk sleeve. "Don't be a fool. We've still got time. You and I can make a run for Washington and . . ."

The door crashed inward with a swirl of dust and the two turned to face the intruder.

The man was tall and thickly built. He had a Walker pistol in his huge and horny hand and his squinted, ink-dot eyes probed the dimness of the room. His heavy, Teutonic face was almost covered by a shaggy, untrimmed beard. The faded red shirt with its big bib and pearl buttons attested that he had come from California, as did his flat-heeled miner's boots.

"Come in," said Michael with a ghost of a bow.

"Is this Santa Rosa?"

"You are correct," replied Michael. "*La hacienda de* Obañon."

The stranger turned and made a come-on gesture with his heavy Walker pistol. "This is the place, Charlie. Come on in!"

Leather creaked and voices rose.

"What the hell do I care where you eat?" roared the stranger. "There must be grub somewhere in these shacks. Go find it. You ain't helpless!"

He turned back to the room and crossed heavily to the table. A choice apple, carefully grown on the rancho, caught the stranger's eye. He picked it up, wiped it on his shirt and sank his yellow fangs into it with a loud crack. Somehow he managed to chew the bite but it impeded his speech for some little time.

Two more men appeared in the doorway.

The stranger again motioned with the pistol. "C'mon. Here's food."

One of the men was squat. His head was large and so were his features, all out of keeping with his size. Though covered with dust, his clothes were loud, consisting of a checkered vest, a yellow suit and a small green hat which he now jerked off and twisted in his hands.

"Mebbe we're intruding, Gus. Mebbe these gents ain't finished their breakfast." He took another turn on his hat and looked nervously at Michael. "Don't mind Gus. He ain't got much manners like Charlie and me."

"Think nothing of it," said Michael with another ghost of a bow, much to the amazement of Klarner. "I shall have a servant bring in more food for you."

"Hell," said Gus, gnawing on the apple, "you speak pretty good English for a damned greaser. Don't he, Mr. Lusby?"

Mr. Lusby gave his hat yet another turn and looked uncomfortable and perspiring. "You don't mind, Gus. If it's too much trouble, *señor.* . . ."

"Think nothing of it," said Michael. "Please be seated."

"My name is Lusby. Julius Lusby, Mr. . . ."

"I am *don* Michael to my friends, Mr. Lusby."

"Sure. Sure. Glad to meetcha, *don* Michael. Look, this is Gus Mueller and this is Charlie Pearson."

Gus did not even bother to nod. He prowled around the big room, still gripping the Walker pistol, opening doors and closing them, bending a calculating eye upon the beautiful Indian rugs and the finely carved, imported furniture.

Charlie Pearson was leaning against the door jamb with his boots crossed. His shirt had once been white linen and his stock was flowing black silk. He had the hard but easy air of the gambler about him.

He eyed Michael suspiciously. Finally, he muttered, "Pleased," and went on picking his teeth.

"Maybe you can tell me where is the boss?" said Mr. Lusby hesitantly.

Gus came to the center of the room and tossed the apple

core out the window. "Sure. We got business around here. Where's the greaser that owns this dump?"

Michael smiled. "Perhaps he has already heard of your coming."

"I get it," said Gus with a harsh laugh. "And he wasn't far from wrong, neither. I suppose you're the major-domo, huh?" And as Michael did not show any signs of doing anything but smiling politely, Gus nudged Mr. Lusby. "Show him the papers."

"Yep," said Charlie. "Show him the papers. We got to make this here thing legal."

Mr. Lusby ran his hands nervously through his pockets and at last located the documents. He edged up to the table, giving the impression of being about to run, and laid several sheets face up on the cloth.

"Since the border's moved," said Mr. Lusby, "all this is United States. I fixed it so the boys could file. And here's the deeds, all ethical and legal, to the Santa Rosa Valley. This ranch house is on it, ain't it?"

"Yes," said Michael.

"There," said Mr. Lusby with a sigh of relief. "I got it done."

Antonio came to the kitchen door and stared in.

"Hey, you," said Gus, "hustle some grub. I could eat a mule."

"*Don* Michael . . ." said Antonio.

"You heard the gentleman, Antonio."

"*Sí, don* Michael," and miserably he withdrew. A moment later came the loud crashing of dishes being thrown about.

Mr. Lusby looked apologetic. "We don't want to put you out none, *señor*. . . ."

"Naw," said Charlie. "But the point is, you'll have to find someplace to sleep. We're takin' over here."

"Naturally," said *don* Michael. "Come, judge."

"Wait a minute," said Mr. Lusby. "Look. We don't know nothing about this place. We don't know where the cows is or nothing. Maybe you want a job, huh?"

"A job?" said Michael.

"Sure," said Mr. Lusby. "You look like a pretty good feller. We'll pay you thirty dollars a month." He added hastily, "But not another nickel!"

"Why, you are too kind," said *don* Michael. "As I am out of employment, I shall be happy to accept such a liberal offer." He gave them a smile, accompanied by a floating gesture of his hands which gave them to understand that he was completely theirs to command. "And now, if you gentlemen will excuse me, I shall show your men where the forage is kept."

"That's the spirit," said Charlie unexpectedly. "When you find out the other gent's got a third ace as his hole card, don't go quittin'. Deal 'em up, I says."

Michael took his silver-encrusted sombrero from the wall and put it on, adjusting the diamond which held the flowing chin thong. He buckled the silver-inlaid pistol about his waist, and so normal did that gesture seem to the three strangers that they failed to note it.

Michael motioned to Judge Klarner and walked out into the hot morning sunlight of the yard.

To find out more about *Six-Gun Caballero* and how you can obtain your copy, go to www.goldenagestories.com.

Glossary

STORIES FROM THE GOLDEN AGE *reflect the words and expressions used in the 1930s and 1940s, adding unique flavor and authenticity to the tales. While a character's speech may often reflect regional origins, it also can convey attitudes common in the day. So that readers can better grasp such cultural and historical terms, uncommon words or expressions of the era, the following glossary has been provided.*

---

batwings: long chaps (leather leggings the cowboy wears to protect his legs) with big flaps of leather. They usually fasten with rings and snaps.

beat, see the: to hear of or to see someone or something better than or surpassing (someone or something else).

caballero: (Spanish) gentleman.

Castilian: a native or inhabitant of Castile, a former kingdom comprising most of Spain.

Chisholm Trail: a cattle trail leading north from San Antonio, Texas, to Abilene, Kansas; used in the late 1800s for about twenty years after the Civil War to drive cattle northward to the railhead of the Kansas Pacific Railway, where they were shipped eastward.

Colt: the cowboy's favorite gun, also known as the Peacemaker. It was the earliest type of revolver, invented and manufactured by Samuel Colt (1814–1862), who revolutionized the firearms industry.

combines: combinations of persons or groups for the furtherance of political, commercial or other interests.

court to, paid: tried to win somebody's love.

cow town: a town at the end of the trail from which cattle were shipped; later applied to towns in the cattle country that depended upon the cowman and his trade for their existence.

coyote: a contemptible person, especially a greedy or dishonest one.

Custer's Last Stand: also known as the Battle of the Little Bighorn, a battle between US Cavalry troops and Native Americans in 1876 near the Little Bighorn River in what is now Montana. The battle was the most famous incident in the Indian Wars, in which a US Cavalry detachment commanded by Lieutenant Colonel George Armstrong Custer was annihilated.

Derringer: a pocket-sized, short-barreled, large-caliber pistol. Named for the US gunsmith Henry Deringer (1786–1868), who designed it.

diggings: living quarters; lodgings.

'dobe: short for adobe; a building constructed with sun-dried bricks made from clay.

don: (Spanish) Mr.; a title of respect before a man's first name.

dragnet: to systematically search for a wanted person.

fastnesses: remote and secluded places; secure places, well protected by natural features.

forty-one or **.41:** Derringer .41-caliber short pistol. Named for the US gunsmith Henry Deringer (1786–1868), who designed it.

G-men: government men; agents of the Federal Bureau of Investigation.

gumbo: soil that turns very sticky and muddy when it becomes wet; found throughout the central US.

hell on skates: also "hell on wheels"; very impressive.

Hickok: James Butler Hickok or better known as Wild Bill Hickok (1837–1876), a legendary figure in the American Old West. After fighting in the Union army during the Civil War, he became a famous army scout and, later, lawman and gunfighter.

hole card: (poker) a playing card dealt face down and not revealed until the showdown.

Holliday: John Henry "Doc" Holliday (1851–1887), an American dentist, gambler and gunfighter of the Old West frontier. He is usually remembered for his associations with the famous marshal of the Arizona Territory, Wyatt Earp, whom he joined in the gunfight at the OK Corral against members of the Clanton gang of suspected cattle rustlers.

hoss: horse.

in arms: up in arms; ready to take action; outraged.

iron: a handgun, especially a revolver.

jasper: a fellow; a guy.

jerk: to preserve (meat, especially beef) by cutting in strips and curing by drying in the sun.

Judge Colt: a Colt designed by Samuel Colt. This was a handgun with a revolving cylinder of chambers allowing six shots to be fired without reloading. Over the years the revolver was given nicknames including "Judge Colt and his jury of six" or "Judge Colt."

KC: Kansas City.

la hacienda de **Obañon:** (Spanish) the ranch of Obañon.

leg-of-mutton silk sleeve: a silk sleeve that is extremely wide over the upper arm and narrow from the elbow to the wrist.

livery stable: a stable that accommodates and looks after horses for their owners.

lynch mob: a group of people who capture and hang someone without legal arrest and trial, because they think the person has committed a crime.

Madre de Dios: (Spanish) Mother of God.

major-domo: a man in charge of a great household, as that of a sovereign; a chief steward.

Masterson: William Barclay "Bat" Masterson (1853–1921), a legendary figure of the American West. He lived an adventurous life, which included stints as a buffalo hunter, US Army scout, gambler, frontier lawman, US marshal and, finally, sports editor and columnist for a New York newspaper.

mean: unimposing or shabby.

mesquite: any of several small spiny trees or shrubs native to the southwestern US and Mexico, and important as plants for bees and forage for cattle.

mow: haymow; the upper floor of a barn or stable used for storing hay.

muy hidalgo: (Spanish) very noble.

neck-reined: guided a horse by pressure of the reins against its neck.

Overland: Sanderson's Overland Stage Company; a well-known firm that ran a mountain stage line that serviced a large portion of southern Colorado and northern New Mexico during the late 1800s.

owl-hoot: outlaw.

Piedmont: a type of horse bred in the Piedmont region, an area of land lying between the Appalachian Mountains and the Atlantic coast.

pitching hole: refers to a hole that provides access to the haymow (the upper floor of a barn or stable used for storing hay). It is used to pitch hay down to the animals.

puncher: a hired hand who tends cattle and performs other duties on horseback.

pushing up prickly pear: variation of "pushing up daisies"; to be dead. A prickly pear is a cactus with flattened, jointed, spiny stems and pear-shaped fruits that are edible in some species.

quirt: 1. a riding whip with a short handle and a braided leather lash. 2. to use a quirt.

ranny: ranahan; a cowboy or top ranch hand.

remuda: a group of saddle horses from which ranch hands pick mounts for the day.

riata: a long, noosed rope used to catch animals.

royal flush: in poker, the highest "flush" or sequence of five consecutive cards of the same suit, including an ace, king, queen, jack and ten.

saddle boot: a close-fitting covering or case for a gun or other weapon that straps to a saddle.

Saint Ignacio: Saint Ignatius of Loyola, a Catholic saint. Used as an exclamation.

sand: courage and determination.

Scheherazade: the female narrator of *The Arabian Nights,* who during one thousand and one adventurous nights saved her life by entertaining her husband, the king, with stories.

serape: a long, brightly colored woolen blanket worn as a cloak by some men from Mexico, Central America and South America.

seven-day wonder: someone or something that causes interest or excitement for a short period but is then quickly forgotten.

sombrero: a Mexican style of hat that was common in the Southwest. It had a high-curved wide brim, a long, loose chin strap and the crown was dented at the top. Like cowboy hats generally, it kept off the sun and rain, fended off the branches and served as a handy bucket or cup.

stock: 1. a collar or a neckcloth fitting like a band around the neck. 2. livestock.

Teutonic: of, pertaining to, or characteristic of the Teutons or Germans; German. (A *Teuton* is a member of a Germanic people or tribe first mentioned in the fourth century BC.)

tinhorn: a gambler of a cheap, flashy, pretentious kind.

Walker pistol: a Colt Walker pistol, originally manufactured in 1847, named after Captain Samuel Hamilton Walker, a renowned national hero who had fought in the Texas-Mexico wars.

willow grate: an open lattice frame for cooking over a fire, made from the tough, pliable branches of a willow tree.

Winchester: an early family of repeating rifles; a single-barreled rifle containing multiple rounds of ammunition. Manufactured by the Winchester Repeating Arms Company, it was widely used in the US during the latter half of the nineteenth century. The 1873 model is often called "the gun that won the West" for its immense popularity at that time, as well as its use in fictional Westerns.

L. Ron Hubbard
in the Golden Age
of Pulp Fiction

*In writing an adventure story
a writer has to know that he is adventuring
for a lot of people who cannot.
The writer has to take them here and there
about the globe and show them
excitement and love and realism.
As long as that writer is living the part of an
adventurer when he is hammering
the keys, he is succeeding with his story.*

*Adventuring is a state of mind.
If you adventure through life, you have a
good chance to be a success on paper.*

*Adventure doesn't mean globe-trotting,
exactly, and it doesn't mean great deeds.
Adventuring is like art.
You have to live it to make it real.*

— *L. RON HUBBARD*

L. Ron Hubbard
and American
Pulp Fiction

B ORN March 13, 1911, L. Ron Hubbard lived a life at
least as expansive as the stories with which he enthralled
a hundred million readers through a fifty-year career.

Originally hailing from Tilden, Nebraska, he spent his
formative years in a classically rugged Montana, replete with
the cowpunchers, lawmen and desperadoes who would later
people his Wild West adventures. And lest anyone imagine
those adventures were drawn from vicarious experience, he
was not only breaking broncs at a tender age, he was also
among the few whites ever admitted into Blackfoot society
as a bona fide blood brother. While if only to round out an
otherwise rough and tumble youth, his mother was that rarity
of her time—a thoroughly educated woman—who introduced
her son to the classics of Occidental literature even before
his seventh birthday.

But as any dedicated L. Ron Hubbard reader will attest, his
world extended far beyond Montana. In point of fact, and as the
son of a United States naval officer, by the age of eighteen he
had traveled over a quarter of a million miles. Included therein
were three Pacific crossings to a then still mysterious Asia, where
he ran with the likes of Her British Majesty's agent-in-place

L. Ron Hubbard, left, at Congressional Airport, Washington, DC, 1931, with members of George Washington University flying club.

for North China, and the last in the line of Royal Magicians from the court of Kublai Khan. For the record, L. Ron Hubbard was also among the first Westerners to gain admittance to forbidden Tibetan monasteries below Manchuria, and his photographs of China's Great Wall long graced American geography texts.

Upon his return to the United States and a hasty completion of his interrupted high school education, the young Ron Hubbard entered George Washington University. There, as fans of his aerial adventures may have heard, he earned his wings as a pioneering barnstormer at the dawn of American aviation. He also earned a place in free-flight record books for the longest sustained flight above Chicago. Moreover, as a roving reporter for *Sportsman Pilot* (featuring his first professionally penned articles), he further helped inspire a generation of pilots who would take America to world airpower.

Immediately beyond his sophomore year, Ron embarked on the first of his famed ethnological expeditions, initially to then untrammeled Caribbean shores (descriptions of which would later fill a whole series of West Indies mystery-thrillers). That the Puerto Rican interior would also figure into the future of Ron Hubbard stories was likewise no accident. For in addition to cultural studies of the island, a 1932–33

LRH expedition is rightly remembered as conducting the first complete mineralogical survey of a Puerto Rico under United States jurisdiction.

There was many another adventure along this vein: As a lifetime member of the famed Explorers Club, L. Ron Hubbard charted North Pacific waters with the first shipboard radio direction finder, and so pioneered a long-range navigation system universally employed until the late twentieth century. While not to put too fine an edge on it, he also held a rare Master Mariner's license to pilot any vessel, of any tonnage in any ocean.

Yet lest we stray too far afield, there is an LRH note at this juncture in his saga, and it reads in part:

"I started out writing for the pulps, writing the best I knew, writing for every mag on the stands, slanting as well as I could."

To which one might add: His earliest submissions date from the summer of 1934, and included tales drawn from true-to-life Asian adventures, with characters roughly modeled on British/American intelligence operatives he had known in Shanghai. His early Westerns were similarly peppered with details drawn from personal experience. Although therein lay a first hard lesson from the often cruel world of the pulps. His first Westerns were soundly rejected as lacking the authenticity of a Max Brand yarn

Capt. L. Ron Hubbard in Ketchikan, Alaska, 1940, on his Alaskan Radio Experimental Expedition, the first of three voyages conducted under the Explorers Club flag.

(a particularly frustrating comment given L. Ron Hubbard's Westerns came straight from his Montana homeland, while Max Brand was a mediocre New York poet named Frederick Schiller Faust, who turned out implausible six-shooter tales from the terrace of an Italian villa).

Nevertheless, and needless to say, L. Ron Hubbard persevered and soon earned a reputation as among the most publishable names in pulp fiction, with a ninety percent placement rate of first-draft manuscripts. He was also among the most prolific, averaging between seventy and a hundred thousand words a month. Hence the rumors that L. Ron Hubbard had redesigned a typewriter for faster keyboard action and pounded out manuscripts on a continuous roll of butcher paper to save the precious seconds it took to insert a single sheet of paper into manual typewriters of the day.

That all L. Ron Hubbard stories did not run beneath said byline is yet another aspect of pulp fiction lore. That is, as publishers periodically rejected manuscripts from top-drawer authors if only to avoid paying top dollar, L. Ron Hubbard and company just as frequently replied with submissions under various pseudonyms. In Ron's case, the

---

A MAN OF MANY NAMES

Between 1934 and 1950, L. Ron Hubbard authored more than fifteen million words of fiction in more than two hundred classic publications. To supply his fans and editors with stories across an array of genres and pulp titles, he adopted fifteen pseudonyms in addition to his already renowned L. Ron Hubbard byline.

Winchester Remington Colt
Lt. Jonathan Daly
Capt. Charles Gordon
Capt. L. Ron Hubbard
Bernard Hubbel
Michael Keith
Rene Lafayette
Legionnaire 148
Legionnaire 14830
Ken Martin
Scott Morgan
Lt. Scott Morgan
Kurt von Rachen
Barry Randolph
Capt. Humbert Reynolds

list included: Rene Lafayette, Captain Charles Gordon, Lt. Scott Morgan and the notorious Kurt von Rachen—supposedly on the lam for a murder rap, while hammering out two-fisted prose in Argentina. The point: While L. Ron Hubbard as Ken Martin spun stories of Southeast Asian intrigue, LRH as Barry Randolph authored tales of

L. Ron Hubbard, circa 1930, at the outset of a literary career that would finally span half a century.

romance on the Western range—which, stretching between a dozen genres is how he came to stand among the two hundred elite authors providing close to a million tales through the glory days of American Pulp Fiction.

In evidence of exactly that, by 1936 L. Ron Hubbard was literally leading pulp fiction's elite as president of New York's American Fiction Guild. Members included a veritable pulp hall of fame: Lester "Doc Savage" Dent, Walter "The Shadow" Gibson, and the legendary Dashiell Hammett—to cite but a few.

Also in evidence of just where L. Ron Hubbard stood within his first two years on the American pulp circuit: By the spring of 1937, he was ensconced in Hollywood, adopting a Caribbean thriller for Columbia Pictures, remembered today as *The Secret of Treasure Island*. Comprising fifteen thirty-minute episodes, the L. Ron Hubbard screenplay led to the most profitable matinée serial in Hollywood history. In accord with Hollywood culture, he was thereafter continually called upon

The 1937 Secret of Treasure Island, *a fifteen-episode serial adapted for the screen by L. Ron Hubbard from his novel,* Murder at Pirate Castle.

to rewrite/doctor scripts—most famously for long-time friend and fellow adventurer Clark Gable.

In the interim—and herein lies another distinctive chapter of the L. Ron Hubbard story—he continually worked to open Pulp Kingdom gates to up-and-coming authors. Or, for that matter, anyone who wished to write. It was a fairly unconventional stance, as markets were already thin and competition razor sharp. But the fact remains, it was an L. Ron Hubbard hallmark that he vehemently lobbied on behalf of young authors—regularly supplying instructional articles to trade journals, guest-lecturing to short story classes at George Washington University and Harvard, and even founding his own creative writing competition. It was established in 1940, dubbed the Golden Pen, and guaranteed winners both New York representation and publication in *Argosy*.

But it was John W. Campbell Jr.'s *Astounding Science Fiction* that finally proved the most memorable LRH vehicle. While every fan of L. Ron Hubbard's galactic epics undoubtedly knows the story, it nonetheless bears repeating: By late 1938, the pulp publishing magnate of Street & Smith was determined to revamp *Astounding Science Fiction* for broader readership. In particular, senior editorial director F. Orlin Tremaine called for stories with a stronger *human element*. When acting editor John W. Campbell balked, preferring his spaceship-driven

104

tales, Tremaine enlisted Hubbard. Hubbard, in turn, replied with the genre's first truly *character-driven* works, wherein heroes are pitted not against bug-eyed monsters but the mystery and majesty of deep space itself—and thus was launched the Golden Age of Science Fiction.

The names alone are enough to quicken the pulse of any science fiction aficionado, including LRH friend and protégé, Robert Heinlein, Isaac Asimov, A. E. van Vogt and Ray Bradbury. Moreover, when coupled with LRH stories of fantasy, we further come to what's rightly been described as the foundation of every modern tale of horror: L. Ron Hubbard's immortal *Fear*. It was rightly proclaimed by Stephen King as one of the very few works to genuinely warrant that overworked term "classic"—as in: *"This is a classic tale of creeping, surreal menace and horror. . . . This is one of the really, really good ones."*

L. Ron Hubbard, 1948, among fellow science fiction luminaries at the World Science Fiction Convention in Toronto.

To accommodate the greater body of L. Ron Hubbard fantasies, Street & Smith inaugurated *Unknown*—a classic pulp if there ever was one, and wherein readers were soon thrilling to the likes of *Typewriter in the Sky* and *Slaves of Sleep* of which Frederik Pohl would declare: *"There are bits and pieces from Ron's work that became part of the language in ways that very few other writers managed."*

And, indeed, at J. W. Campbell Jr.'s insistence, Ron was regularly drawing on themes from the Arabian Nights and so introducing readers to a world of genies, jinn, Aladdin and Sinbad—all of which, of course, continue to float through cultural mythology to this day.

At least as influential in terms of post-apocalypse stories was L. Ron Hubbard's 1940 *Final Blackout*. Generally acclaimed as the finest anti-war novel of the decade and among the ten best works of the genre ever authored—here, too, was a tale that would live on in ways few other writers imagined.

Hence, the later Robert Heinlein verdict: "Final Blackout *is as perfect a piece of science fiction as has ever been written.*"

Like many another who both lived and wrote American pulp adventure, the war proved a tragic end to Ron's sojourn in the pulps. He served with distinction in four theaters and was highly decorated for commanding corvettes in the North Pacific. He was also grievously wounded in combat, lost many a close friend and colleague and thus resolved to say farewell to pulp fiction and devote himself to what it had supported these many years—namely, his serious research.

Portland, Oregon, 1943; L. Ron Hubbard, captain of the US Navy subchaser PC 815.

But in no way was the LRH literary saga at an end, for as he wrote some thirty years later, in 1980:

"Recently there came a period when I had little to do. This was novel in a life so crammed with busy years, and I decided to amuse myself by writing a novel that was pure *science fiction."*

That work was *Battlefield Earth: A Saga of the Year 3000*. It was an immediate *New York Times* bestseller and, in fact, the first international science fiction blockbuster in decades. It was not, however, L. Ron Hubbard's magnum opus, as that distinction is generally reserved for his next and final work: The 1.2 million word *Mission Earth*.

> **Final Blackout**
> *is as perfect a piece of science fiction as has ever been written.*
>
> —Robert Heinlein

How he managed those 1.2 million words in just over twelve months is yet another piece of the L. Ron Hubbard legend. But the fact remains, he did indeed author a ten-volume *dekalogy* that lives in publishing history for the fact that each and every volume of the series was also a *New York Times* bestseller.

Moreover, as subsequent generations discovered L. Ron Hubbard through republished works and novelizations of his screenplays, the mere fact of his name on a cover signaled an international bestseller. . . . Until, to date, sales of his works exceed hundreds of millions, and he otherwise remains among the most enduring and widely read authors in literary history. Although as a final word on the tales of L. Ron Hubbard, perhaps it's enough to simply reiterate what editors told readers in the glory days of American Pulp Fiction:

He writes the way he does, brothers, because he's been there, seen it and done it!

THE STORIES FROM THE GOLDEN AGE

Your ticket to adventure starts here with the Stories from
the Golden Age collection by master storyteller L. Ron Hubbard.
These gripping tales are set in a kaleidoscope of exotic locales and brim
with fascinating characters, including some of the
most vile villains, dangerous dames and brazen heroes
you'll ever get to meet.

The entire collection of over one hundred and fifty stories is being
released in a series of eighty books and audiobooks.
For an up-to-date listing of available titles,
go to www.goldenagestories.com.

AIR ADVENTURE

FAR-FLUNG ADVENTURE

SEA ADVENTURE

TALES FROM THE ORIENT

MYSTERY

WESTERN

The Baron of Coyote River	*Man for Breakfast*
Blood on His Spurs	*The No-Gun Gunhawk*
Boss of the Lazy B	*The No-Gun Man*
Branded Outlaw	*The Ranch That No One Would Buy*
Cattle King for a Day	*Reign of the Gila Monster*
Come and Get It	*Ride 'Em, Cowboy*
Death Waits at Sundown	*Ruin at Rio Piedras*
Devil's Manhunt	*Shadows from Boot Hill*
The Ghost Town Gun-Ghost	*Silent Pards*
Gun Boss of Tumbleweed	*Six-Gun Caballero*
Gunman!	*Stacked Bullets*
Gunman's Tally	*Stranger in Town*
The Gunner from Gehenna	*Tinhorn's Daughter*
Hoss Tamer	*The Toughest Ranger*
Johnny, the Town Tamer	*Under the Diehard Brand*
King of the Gunmen	*Vengeance Is Mine!*
The Magic Quirt	*When Gilhooly Was in Flower*